DANCE
OF
THE
DEMON

BY SANDRA FENDLER

This book is dedicated to my mother, whose life was never the same after the tragic loss of her son. Thank you for always being there for my brother and me with a listening ear, a caring smile, and wise words.

CURSE OF THE CHINDI SERIES

Curse of the Chindi
Dance of the Demon

ACKNOWLEDGEMENTS

This book is published in tribute to my family and friends. A special thanks goes to my two sons, who gave me the inspiration and determination to write this novel. I also wish to thank my long-time friend Nancy Shelton for her input and support. I sincerely appreciate the guidance and assistance Pat Richmond and Carol Osman Brown provided with the final stages of my manuscript.

Additional thanks to artist Rock Newcomb for the photographic image of his painting, "Dances with Demons," featured on the cover of this book.

PROLOGUE

In truth, a clear motive for my brother's murder may never be discovered. The person(s) responsible may never be known. *Dance of the Demon* is not about revenge, but finding justice and the settling of accounts.

Revenge weakens one's soul, and it quickly becomes a waste of time and energy. Guided by my mother's philosophy, that out of misery comes enlightenment, I have decided to resolve the mystery once and for all.

With the aid of my new husband, Clint, I begin to investigate the strange circumstances surrounding the crime. In following my instincts, I am not far off the mark. Call it a gut reaction or a sixth sense, but I believe that our intuition always leads us to the truth.

Murder creates fear because it makes us aware of our own mortality and vulnerability. Through my faith and determination, I will overcome this personal crisis that has become my own version of hell.

Sarah Simms
Shi-da-zii (little sister)

CHAPTER I

Dreams do come true, but so do your worst nightmares. For five years I'd been searching for answers. Who had murdered my brother, Clayton? And why? Armed with my laptop, I decided it was time to retreat to my favorite haunt, a tiny resort area on the outskirts of Puerto Vallarta, Mexico. *The Mexican Riviera will be perfect at this time of year*, I thought, as I packed the last of my tee shirts and shorts in my suitcase. "Don't worry, I'll be back!" I yelled to the locals as they passed by me in their trucks.

I drove to Phoenix Sky Harbor International airport. As I waited in the international lobby of Aero Mexico airlines, I couldn't help but notice the tall, ruggedly handsome gentleman.

"Good morning, ma'am," he said, tipping his white Stetson as he sat down beside me.

It had been so long since I had felt a physical attraction to a man. At least now I knew I was still alive after the past few dark years.

"I see you're reading a book about the Southwest Native American culture," he said as he glanced at the manuscript cover of *Secrets of a Haunted Trading Post*.

"Yes, I am. But how did you know?"

He smiled. "My first clue was the cover, with its photographic image of a trading post complete with Navajo signage. I'm also familiar with the Navajo language; it's part of my heritage."

I would never have guessed it. He reminded me of a Texas Ranger more than an Indian, although it wouldn't have surprised me to learn he was both.

As we boarded the plane, he turned to me.

"Since it isn't full, would you mind if I join you?"

"Not at all." I moved over to the seat by the window. "Have you ever lived on the Indian reservation?" I asked out of curiosity.

"Not for a long time," he answered. "I'm from Texas. I'm actually a Texas Ranger."

I knew it!

"I ended up taking an early retirement, thanks to the fellow that shattered my knee." He rubbed his left pant leg. "Luckily, it didn't do any permanent damage."

"I hope you didn't let that scoundrel get away with it, and that he received the justice he earned," I said heatedly. "If Walker Texas Ranger had anything to say about it, you can bet that guy would be in jail."

Not like in my brother's case, I silently lamented.

"Apparently you're familiar with the show."

I smiled. "It's my favorite."

"I'm sorry," he said, reaching over to shake my hand. "My name is Clint Walkerman. I'm known as Walker for short, but I'm no relation to the movie star," he added.

Too bad, I thought.

As we got to talking, I explained that my brother had been killed on the Navajo Indian Reservation and that I had written a book about the murder.

"You have?" he asked. "Where can I find a copy? I'd like to read it... And since I now know the author, perhaps you'd sign it for me?"

"Whoa! Not so fast, cowboy," I chuckled. "The book is written, but it's not yet in print. As a matter of fact, I've brought the manuscript with me to finalize it for the publisher."

He seemed interested, so I told him more about my brother's disappearance. "It was the most stressful time of my life...I remember how it took days for us to find someone who would accept jurisdiction over the matter. I didn't know my brother was already dead."

To my surprise, I found myself telling him all about the *Chindi*. "It's a bit mystifying, I know..."

"Not at all. My grandparents warned me about the evils of the *Chindi*, but I never experienced it myself."

"I don't even like talking about it," I said.

He seemed interested in the case, though, so I continued.

"It was a mess from the start...The Apache County Sheriff's Office seemed to think there wasn't any wrongdoing on its part—even though one of their deputies, John Morgan, deliberately concealed and destroyed crucial evidence. Even though that same deputy was served with a restraining order that was issued against him by my brother, he somehow became involved in my brother's murder investigation. I just couldn't believe that this same deputy ended up being the head honcho in charge of the case."

"After being in my line of work for twenty-five years, nothing surprises me."

"It's a wound that's festered for years," I confessed. "One that will probably never heal. It wasn't long after my brother's murder that I received a threatening phone call. My memory is a bit fuzzy as to when it occurred, but that's not important. What matters is the message, and I remember that clearly. It was definitely an ominous threat. And then there was the fire...It's a bit mind-boggling when I sit down and think about it after all this time. If only we could go back and rewrite our lives..."

"If I were you, I'd try not to dwell on it."

"What are your plans when we get to Mexico?" I decided to take his advice and change the topic.

"I'm really not sure. I recently purchased a villa on the ocean, and I plan to spend time just reading and perhaps doing a little deep-sea fishing. I'd love for you to see it, though. Besides, it could use a woman's touch…Oh, sorry. That sounded a bit presumptuous on my part."

"Not at all. I'd be delighted to see it. I'm a frustrated decorator at heart."

"What are *your* plans?" he inquired.

"A friend loaned me a place she has down here. From the second-story balcony, it's a 200-foot drop to the ocean below. I think I'll just become a beachcomber and soak up all the splendors of nature. Ever since I moved from the city to the country, my life has changed. Instead of trying to make a difference in the world, I've concentrated on relationships with the people, plants, and animals closest to me. I've made friends with cactus wrens, rabbits, and all the little critters that scamper about the property. I wasn't prepared for the feeling of loss I experienced when my brother died, so I turned to writing. That's when I really discovered my passion. Sometimes we think we know what our contribution to the world is, only to discover accidentally that it is something else entirely."

I paused, embarrassed to be rambling on to a complete stranger. But he didn't seem to mind. His hazel eyes met mine for a moment, and then shifted to something far away.

"I won't pretend to know how you feel, but I can sympathize. My wife always wanted me to retire. She was afraid that I would be killed in the line of duty. Instead, she was the one who stepped into the path of a stray bullet. I have never gotten over it, and I probably never will—until I find the murderer. That's one of the reasons I'm retiring, so that I can do a little detective work on my own."

I was stunned to learn that an unsolved murder also marred my new friend's life.

"Would you like something to drink before lunch?" the flight attendant interrupted as she leaned over the aisle.

"I would love a margarita," I said, grateful to leave the subject of death.

We continued chatting over cocktails and lunch.

"I remember back when I was a flight attendant, first-class service included delicacies like pheasant under glass served on real china, not to mention the six other courses," I said after taking a bite of my stale lunch roll.

"You used to be a stewardess?"

"Yes, many years ago."

"That's funny. I was just thinking of getting a small plane, although not *too* small. For one thing, it has to be able to fly across the ocean. I still have business in the States, you see. With any luck, I should have a little four-seat Piper Cherokee in a few weeks."

This was too good to be true.

"You're a pilot?"

"Yes, ma'am, and I may be in need of a copilot."

I was almost tempted to tell him that I had taken a few flying lessons. *Almost,* but not quite.

"Do you like this part of Mexico?" he inquired as our plane approached the coastline.

"Yes, I love Puerto Vallarta. I used to visit quite often. In fact, at one point in my life, I practically lived here. I remember when the airport was located on the other side of town and they used to shoo the chickens and cows off the runway."

The sun was streaming in through the windows as we landed.

"I think it's going to be a beautiful day." Clint smiled with his eyes. "I'd be happy to drive you to your accommodations," he said. "I keep a little car at the airport."

I accepted, and as soon as we landed, he helped me with my carry-on bags and escorted me to the terminal.

"If you'll wait here," he said, motioning me to a vacant bench outside the terminal. "I'll go get the car."

Within a few moments, an open-air jeep pulled up to the curb. "I almost didn't recognize you," I said. "What happened to your snow-white hat?" He was wearing an old, brown leather gaucho hat now.

"This one gives me more character. Don't you think?"

"You look like a Mexican Caballero, if that's what you mean."

"A hat is a badge of distinction. A hundred or so years ago, a person could tell where a man came from just by the shape of his hat. Besides, sweaty old cowboy hats are becoming quite fashionable these days. But a hat only becomes a good hat after you've slept under the stars in it and watered your horse out of it."

"Whatever. You still look like a Mexican cowboy to me. The place where I'll be staying is called Villa Verde; it's named after the owner, Mrs. Green. I hope I can find it after all these years."

After we left the airport, we wound our way through the main part of town.

"Would you like to stop and have a real margarita?" he smiled. "There's a quaint café that's located on the bank of the river. It's just a few miles from here."

"I can't refuse an offer like that." I smiled back.

From a table by the window, I could see the peaceful rolling river. "I never knew this place existed," I said while sipping the best margarita I'd ever had.

As we sat there enjoying our drinks, I saw our waiter shinny up a tall coconut palm and pluck a coconut from the tree.

"If you think their margaritas are good, wait until you taste their coco locos!"

We spent an enjoyable afternoon talking.

"I suppose I'd better be getting you home," he said as he looked at his watch. "Will you join me for dinner tonight?"

"I'd love to!"

On the way back, we drove past Gringo Gulch, where two Mexican ladies were doing their laundry in the river. "There's no mistaking it, you definitely know you're on foreign soil," I said as we continued along the dusty narrow road.

He drove the jeep almost to my front doorstep.

"May I help you with your bags?"

"Yes, but I must warn you: there are two flights of stairs."

"I don't mind."

We trudged up to the second floor. From the open room, we could see for miles. There were no walls or windows to obstruct the view of the ocean.

"This is really unique," he said, as we stood in the shaded recess. "But aren't you afraid to stay here alone?"

"Not really. The only intruders I've ever encountered were Hughie, Dewey, and Louie; three fruit bats. And they've never harmed me."

We walked out to the steps that seemed to vanish like a staircase into the sea. "This place doesn't seem very safe to me," Clint said as he peered out over the edge at the two hundred or more steps that led to the rippled sand on the beach below. "It wouldn't take much effort for someone to climb those steps and scale these walls...But, I'll trust your judgment. I'll pick you up tonight at eight."

After I closed the door, I thought I heard the doorbell ring. *That's odd*, I thought. Expecting to see Clint, I opened it with a smile, but no one was there. It must have been my imagination.

A few minutes before eight, I heard the doorbell ring again. This time I kept the chain on the door when I opened it. "Who is it?" I asked.

"It's Clint," a voice called through the opening.

"I'm glad to see you're being cautious at least," he said as he entered. "Oh my, don't you look beautiful?"

I was wearing a long Mexican skirt and a low-cut Mexican peasant blouse. Then he grinned. "If it wasn't for your blonde hair, you could pass for a Mexican señorita."

"Touché," I replied. "Now we're even."

He hugged me affectionately, and then asked if I was ready. "I have a beautiful evening planned."

And he did.

It was such a romantic place. I felt like I was in the middle of the Garden of Eden with all the succulent trees, plants, and ferns. There were cascading waterfalls, emerald pools, and verdant patches of luxurious grass sprinkled with areas of wildflowers. It truly was idyllic.

I couldn't resist ordering the restaurant's special, roasted salmon and spinach with a red wine demi-glace. Clint ordered the lobster, along with a very special bottle of Dom Pérignon wine.

"There's nothing quite as soothing as water trickling from a waterfall," I said as I watched it spilling from a rock garden into a blue lagoon. "It's almost hypnotic."

"Earlier in the day, you mentioned how much you like Puerto Vallarta."

"Yes, I love the tropical climate. It's such a contrast to the desert."

"Let's take a walk on the beach after dinner. Perhaps I can convince you to stay."

A fine mist of spray was rolling off the ocean, leaving a haze in the air. We kicked our shoes off, leaving them on the patio of the restaurant. Together we walked barefoot in the sand.

The *Chindi* seemed far away.

Later in the evening, we stopped at a nightclub where Mexican dancers were performing. One of them was wearing a skirt just like mine, and Clint laughed.

"Look over there," I nudged him. A Mexican cowboy was wearing a brown leather gaucho hat—just like his!

"It's inevitable. We're obviously meant for each other. We're two of a kind," he said.

Later we drove back to my little villa, and after we ascended the two flights of stairs, Clint stood stubbornly by the door. "I'm really concerned about your safety."

"Don't worry. I'll be fine."

"Just the same. If there's anything you need, don't hesitate to call, even if it's in the middle of the night." He handed me his card. "How about breakfast tomorrow? I have a Mexican housekeeper who fixes the best huevos rancheros."

"Sounds good to me."

"Until then…" He held out his arms.

"I want you to know you're making my trip very special," I told him.

"I hope so."

"Thank you." I smiled as I closed the door.

I had no sooner turned around than I thought I heard someone at the door. *Not this again.* I opened it cautiously, but it was only Clint.

"I forgot to mention that I'd love to read your book. Would it be all right if I took it home with me?"

"By all means." I reached for the manuscript on the entry table.

"I'm a voracious reader," he said. "I'll have it finished by tonight."

"See you in the morning."

What a whirlwind romance, I thought as I closed the door. I could feel myself tingling with anticipation.

That night as I got ready for bed, I thought I heard the echolocation of the bats. I wondered if they would remember me. They used to fly in and out of the open rooms. It was odd that I didn't see them.

As I lay on the bed with a thin sheet pulled over me, I felt the soft ocean breezes caressing my face. I realized later that I must have fallen asleep…

It must be a dream, I thought, as I felt the cool, fluttering wings above me. The sensation beckoned me into a deeper sleep.

I may have been unconscious, but somehow I knew that something bad was about to happen. I opened my eyes, but I couldn't believe what was in front of me. A bat was hovering.

Somewhere in the back of my mind, I remembered that a bat often anesthetizes its victim by fluttering the wings of its forearms before it bites. I fought it off for all I was worth. Then I ran and hid behind a chair. In its flurry of rage, the bat bared its teeth at me.

And then it flew away.

"That's it," I told the room. "I'm not staying here anymore. I'm going to a hotel. Clint is *not* going to believe this," I muttered as I dialed his number.

"Clint!" I said as he answered the phone. "It looks like Hughie, Dewey, and Louie didn't remember me after all."

"Sarah, is that you?"

"Yes." I started to cry. "I've just been attacked by a bat."

"Are you all right?"

"I think so," I said. "Although in the fracas, I may have sprained my wrist."

"I'll be right over."

I quickly threw on some jeans and my favorite tank top that buttoned up the back. My wrist hurt even more as I fastened it.

By then, Clint was at my door.

"I don't see any marks on your neck or face," he said as he walked in and kissed my forehead.

"I assume he was just getting ready to bite me."

"You're coming home with me."

"Oh, no."

"Oh, *yes*. You're not staying here. I've been reading your book. There's no telling what weird events might happen next. Did it ever occur to you that the *Chindi* may have caused this to happen?" When I didn't immediately reply, he went on. "My, you're stubborn. You must have been quite a handful growing up."

"All right, all right," I finally said, grabbing the night bag which I hadn't completely unpacked. "Let me get a few more items, and then we can go."

We drove through the elaborate, wrought iron entrance. Behind the high wall was an old rambling Spanish hacienda. *How could he afford all this? Was he a drug dealer on the side?* What I actually said was that it seemed a suitable place for a Mexican cowboy.

The exterior of the house had a red tile roof and soaring arches. A colorful mosaic floor complimented the painted murals in the grand foyer.

"This is lovely," I said, pausing to admire a statue of one of the patron saints displayed in its own special nook.

"It's been in my family for years. It actually came out of a church."

"We obviously have the same taste. I have a statue of Our Lady of Guadeloupe. It's said she watches over the family she's with. Imagine what my life would have been like *without* her blessings!"

We toured the main part of the house. The decor was both rustic and elegant, with antique watering cans, urns, and pedestals giving it an eclectic look. As we walked through the west wing of the house, Clint turned to me. "Each of the five guest rooms has its very own fireplace," he said. "Take your pick."

A Texas Ranger with *five* guest rooms!

I decided on one with its own private balcony. Behind the sliding glass doors there was a small seating area. The patio was bricked and had a little trellis covered with bougainvillea. Everywhere I looked, there were potted plants and flowers. There was even a hanging flower box on the rail. "These are absolutely gorgeous," I said as I stood in the little alcove admiring them.

He smiled at me. "If it's flowers you like, there's plenty."

From the end of the alcove, we stepped out into a beautiful garden.

"Would you like a nightcap before we retire?"

"I think I could use one," I admitted.

He directed me to an outdoor courtyard.

"We'll have breakfast out here tomorrow. If you wake up early enough, perhaps we can even watch the sunrise together."

"What a magnificent place you have. It's almost like being on vacation in a five-star resort."

"Thanks, I've been really lucky in my investments."

As we talked, it became apparent that Clint wasn't a money-laundering drug dealer. Two of the world's largest oil companies were interested in some of the land he owned in southern Texas, which contained crude oil.

His friend, Professor Farrari, a geologist and archaeologist, had advised him to team up with ConocoPhillips Co. as it evaluated the property and prepared to launch drilling operations. The company had granted him a sizeable percentage stake in the southern oil field, giving him the funds with which to invest. He'd also had an interest in Amoco when it merged with British Petroleum in 1998.

There was an outdoor bar tucked under a thatched-roof *palapa* in the middle of the patio. As I propped myself up on a barstool, he reached for a glass from behind the well-stocked bar and fixed me a tropical cocktail flavored with flowers.

"I didn't know nasturtiums were edible," I confessed, but he assured me they were.

"I'm feeling a little tired," I said as I finished my drink.

"Then let me escort you to your room."

We walked along the main path that led back to the house, and then down a long corridor.

"Is your sore wrist going to need help with all those buttons?" he asked as we arrived at my room.

"I might have some trouble unfastening them…"

"Then let me assist you," he said as the straps of my shirt slipped provocatively off my shoulders.

He softly kissed the back of my neck.

"Let's see how this goes," I hedged. "It's been awhile since I've thought about romance."

"I'd be the happiest man alive if you'd stay in Puerto Vallarta," he said. "I guess I have eight days to charm you. Maybe the answer will come to you by then."

The next morning, we convened on the outside terrace. "How was your night?" he asked as he reached over and kissed me. "Did you sleep well?"

"Almost *too* well." I kissed him back. "I didn't have my usual menagerie of pets to wake me up."

"We can fix that." He called over a Mexican hybrid gray wolf named Callista.

She looked at me through eyes that reflected a bit of red from my shirt.

"Don't worry, she's friendly."

"Yeah, right. Just like the bats."

As we sat under the shade of an umbrella table facing the ocean, his housekeeper set out a plate of fresh papaya. He offered me a slice. "Juanita is like a member of the family," he said as he introduced us.

"Would you like some coffee?" she asked.

"Yes, please. I just drink it black."

We sipped hibiscus juice and admired the view of the ocean. Callista never took her eyes off me.

It wasn't long before Juanita brought our huevos rancheros.

"These look delicious," I said, ready to dig in.

"She uses a recipe that goes back for generations. What makes it so special is that she uses three types of chili peppers in her ingredients."

We spent the afternoon together, and several more after that. After numerous nights of Latin dancing, I was forced to declare a truce.

"I know it takes two to tango," I said, "but I think I'm ready to call it a night."

We made our way down the long corridor to my room. "I'll let you rest," Clint laughed as I plunked down on the bed. He looked tantalizingly handsome in the moonlight shining through the window.

"Let me open this window for you. Listening to the ocean should put you to sleep."

He leaned over and kissed me good night, then turned and closed the door behind him. The room grew dark. I lay there thinking of Clint and his kiss as I drifted toward sleep.

Suddenly I saw two slanted eyes glowing in the dark. *I hope that window has a screen on it*, I thought, as I continued to watch the greenish-amber eyes peering at me.

What happened after that, I was never quite sure. It could have been the effect of the wine I had earlier. All I know is that when I focused my eyes, the screen was in a twisted heap on the floor with a hole ripped through its center. Clint was standing over me.

"Good God! What happened?"

"I don't know. The last thing I remember is seeing these fiery eyes…You don't suppose Callista did this, do you? She's been watching me all day."

"If she did, she must have had a reason."

"But I didn't do anything to provoke her!"

"I know. That's what bothers me."

"What's that supposed to mean?"

He didn't answer my question, only asked one of his own. "Did you see anything else that seemed unusual?"

"Not really."

"Here, let me help you up."

My wrist was sore again, and I hurt all over.

"You're sleeping with me tonight."

I didn't object as I followed Clint to his room.

"Sarah, you've been alone through all this and have had no help. Well, now I'm here to help you. These are issues that need to be resolved. We need to talk."

Just then the phone rang. Clint ran over and grabbed the receiver. "It's Ranger Estes from my office."

I realized Clint must have told his former boss about my brother's homicide and suggested that the police were involved in some sort of cover-up.

"Estes says your brother's case has been cleared."

"What?" I said, flabbergasted.

Hanging up the phone, he went on to explain. "In police parlance, that's just another way of saying the case has been closed. And just because a case is cleared, it doesn't mean the perpetrator goes to prison. A case is cleared in police logs even if there is no arrest but police establish to their satisfaction who the bad guy is."

"Well, that's *great* news! As if I'm not frustrated enough," I replied sarcastically.

"Personally, I don't see how they were able to clear the case without any proof. Or without even having a trial, because the person who was accused of committing the crime is already dead, killed by a self-inflicted gunshot wound to the head."

"Well, that's very convenient, isn't it?" I asked, grimacing.

"Don't worry. What goes around comes around."

"That's really profound," I quipped.

"It is."

Clint walked back over to the place where I had been standing. "I realize it hasn't been easy coping with the agony of no answers and the frustration of a justice system that wasn't there for you. My concern now is for *you*, though. I'm afraid that you may have bitten off more than you can chew," he continued in a worried voice. "The people involved in your brother's murder are not going to be happy to learn that you've written a book. They may even go so far as to follow you down here to try to prevent you from publishing it. I just don't want to see you end up in some deep abyss."

I looked at him, genuinely startled. He noted my expression but kept talking.

"I've read parts of your book over and over. It's hard to believe that everything you wrote is true, but the fact that it's a true story makes it even more impactful. There were times when I just wanted to wring somebody's neck. But now it's time to come to terms with your grief. You need to focus on the positive, and let whoever or whatever is hell-bent on destroying you become ensnared in their own trap. Believe it or not, just shifting your viewpoint and thoughts can lift a curse. It's all your state of mind."

A corner of my mouth turned up in a smile. "If only it were that easy."

"Look at it as turning a page, or writing a new chapter," he said. "I try to live each day like it's a new chapter, and I do, but that doesn't mean I don't intend to end the unfinished chapter of my life."

I knew he was referring to his wife's death.

"You're a strong spirit, Sarah. Don't be afraid to reflect on the journey that brought you to this moment. Give it a voice. Everyone has a story to tell deep down, and yours must be told. We don't find meaning from challenges or misery. We find meaning in how we face those challenges."

I turned a deaf ear as soon as Clint started talking about challenges. Then I surprised myself by responding. "Step up to the challenge? Why not just invite the devil into a duel? It's not an easy feat you're talking about. You don't know what I'm up against. Do you realize I've evoked the *Chindi*, the leader of all underworld figures and the ruler of hell, as an adversary?"

"Trust me, Sarah. We can solve this murder. In the end, justice will prevail."

"I hope you're right, Clint," I shuddered. I couldn't hide the trace of doubt in my voice.

"Most of your story hasn't been written yet. The end is up to you."

Before going to bed, Clint loaded his pistol. At first we slept back to back. Then Clint rolled over and held me. It felt good to have his arms around me. It was enough for now.

"Wake up, Clint," I whispered urgently sometime later. "Did you hear that low, eerie hum?"

"It's probably just the crickets chirping," he mumbled.

"No, Clint. It's more of a growl."

I was drawn to the window. The wind was blowing between the palm fronds and the air had a pungent quality. The floodlights cast long eerie shadows on the grass.

"I hate to say it," I said calmly. "But I think there's a ghost in your yard. Its skin looks as wrinkled and brown as on the day of its burial."

"That's just the gardener," he laughed. "He sometimes patrols the property late at night."

"Clint! Get up!" I said angrily. Just then, I saw the wolf in the clearing, its mouth open in a terrifying howl.

"I hope you heard *that*!"

He jumped up. "That's Callista's cry, and she's not just howling at the moon." He grabbed his gun and ran out of the house.

What followed next was bizarre. I saw Callista leap into the air and then into the bushes. Beyond the canopy of trees, between the patches of light, all that was visible was a twisted form encased in suffocating rags and bandages that resembled an ancient mummy. I wondered if it was the *Chindi*?

A gunshot rang out. I flinched and ran outside.

"What in God's name was that?" I yelled to Clint, who was kneeling beside Callista.

"I honestly don't know," he said, "but apparently Callista was no match for whatever it was. You were such a brave little girl," he said as he petted her.

Then I saw the gash on her throat and chest.

"You stay with her." Clint instructed me. "I'll go get the vet. I shouldn't be more than a few minutes."

I cradled her in my lap and hugged her as best I could. "You're going to be all right," I assured her.

She lifted her head as if she were trying to tell me something.

"You saw it, didn't you? That thing bound in rags."

She licked my hand. "I'll take it that means yes."

Then I heard the unmistakable sound of thunder. Then it came again, this time in the form of a rumble and crack. Just what we needed now...a storm.

"Wolves are very territorial and will fight off any intruding wolves," the vet said when he examined her, "but for the life of me, I can't imagine what she met up with. Whatever it was, it had the strength of a bear. Can you help me get her into my truck? She's definitely going to require surgery."

Clint retrieved a small flatbed wagon. We lifted her onto it and pulled her gently toward the house. From there we transferred her to the vet's truck, and he drove off.

Afterward, Clint and I searched the property for any clues to explain what might have happened. The only thing that was left at the scene was a piece of gauze, and what looked like parchment paper. "What do you suppose this is?" I asked as I examined it.

"I have no idea."

We walked through the bushes toward the front entrance of the house.

"I don't think she went this far," I said.

"For her sake, maybe it's just as well..." Suddenly Clint grabbed me and shielded my body with his own. Then I saw one of the most frightening things I'd ever seen. A man's body was dangling upside down; his left leg caught up on one of the iron spires of the gateway. "Oh my God!" I screamed. "Is that the gardener?"

"I think so," Clint said quietly. "Go on back to the house. There's a list of emergency numbers by the phone in the kitchen. Call the police. In the meantime, I'll see if there's anything I can do for him."

I ran back to the house, but I couldn't stop shaking as I picked up the phone. I was trembling so badly that I needed two hands to hold it. "Dear God, please don't let this be true."

The line was dead.

Suddenly the window next to where I was standing blew open. "Oh, Clint! Where are you?" I shouted as I struggled to close it.

Then the lights went out. *Don't panic*, I said to myself. Once I was able to manage the fear, my survival instincts kicked in. *I just need to find a weapon.* I rummaged through the kitchen drawers and found a knife. In reality, I knew a knife was no defense against a spirit, but this was *not* reality.

It was just before dawn, but still very dark, especially with the approaching storm. As I stood in the dim interior, I thought I saw a shadow in the hallway. I peered around the corner. There was no one there, but I did hear some suspicious sounds.

I started down the hallway. I had not been in the east end of the house before. I passed by two bedrooms. When I came to the next room, the door was closed. As I opened it, I was relieved to see Juanita. She was lighting a row of candles at a homemade altar. She gasped when she saw me standing there holding a knife.

"Don't worry, Juanita. I'm not going to hurt you. It's just that there is something very weird going on."

"I know, that's why I'm praying. Something terrible is going to happen."

"Would you like to come back to the kitchen with me? You might feel safer."

"No, *gracias*. I will stay here and pray."

I heard her door squeak to a close. The hallway grew even darker. Why hadn't I thought to bring a flashlight? Maybe I could borrow one of Juanita's candles. I turned and went back, knocking softly on her door.

"Juanita," I whispered. There was no answer, so I knocked a little louder. Then I tried the doorknob. It was locked. "Juanita!" I screamed. My voice echoed off the three-inch-thick walls. There was no response.

Slowly I backed away from the door. Across the hall, there was another bedroom. I thought I heard something behind me, but when I turned around, I felt like I had been hurled into another dimension. Lurching out at me, protruding out of the bedroom, was a hideously gaping mouth, its lips spread in a howl. Of what? Fear? Rage? A plea for help? I had no way of knowing.

I started blindly running down the hall. When I came to an opening, I felt a terrible jolt. Instinctively I lifted the arm that was holding the knife.

"My God! What are you doing?"

It was Clint. I fainted into his arms. When I woke up, the lights were on and he was talking with the police.

"Are you feeling any better?" asked the officer. "Now that you're awake, would you like to tell us about what happened?"

"It was so weird," I said, still a bit baffled by it all.

"You're not the only one who's confused."

The police confirmed that Juanita was dead. "It appears that she died of natural causes, probably from a heart attack."

"And the gardener?"

"He'll be all right. In trying to escape from whatever was in the bushes, he obviously wasn't able to scale the fence as well as he thought he could."

Clint sat on the edge of the bed and tried to comfort me. I looked up at him with weary eyes. "I have seen the enemy."

I pictured that terrifying apparition with its hollow eyes and broken teeth beneath the painted headdress. "Strangely, it looked a lot like a Kachina I once saw at a gift shop in Sedona, Arizona. If that was the *Chindi*, it looked as if it was suffering a fate worse than death!"

I turned to the officer. "I'm sorry I wasn't more helpful."

Then I heard the sound of sirens as the ambulances pulled away.

"I guess that's all we can do tonight." The officer picked up his hat. "See you mañana, Walker."

"*Buenos noches.*"

For the rest of the night, Clint tried to console me. "I know you've been through a lot, but I think we need to get to the bottom of this. We need to find out why these things are happening. I hate to cut your vacation short, but I'd like us to fly to the reservation tomorrow. I have a friend who's a Hopi priest. He might be able to provide us with some answers."

"I thought you were Navajo."

"I am, at least part Navajo...So what, we're both Native Americans, aren't we?" He laughed, then turned quickly serious as he looked into my eyes. "Sarah, as I said before, I want you to know that from now on, you're not alone. I'm with you. Our meeting on the plane feels like destiny to me. I know it's only been a few days, but I care for you. And I think you're beginning to care for me, too. Maybe fate has brought us together so we can find our answers together."

"I don't know if I like that idea," I said crankily. "Every time I search for answers, there always seems to be deadly consequences."

CHAPTER II

When I woke later in the morning, I was apprehensive. Usually I was willing to take a risk, but second-guessing what the *Chindi* were doing was another matter. I looked up to see Clint standing in the open doorway with a cup of coffee.

"Take your time getting up," he said. "There's no need to rush. I'd like to take my new mare for a quick ride before we go. White Lightning hasn't had much exercise lately. While I'm out, I'll ride over to Juanita's family to give my condolences and explain to them why we won't be here for the funeral."

He set my coffee on the night table. "We can leave after I finish up here."

"I'm not quite sure I want to go to the reservation and stir up more trouble."

"What do we have to lose?"

Only our lives, I thought.

"What if I were to tell you that we could do a check out on the new plane?"

"You got it?"

"Yes."

Wasn't it funny how life could take its own turns? I never would have dreamed that I'd meet a Prince Charming at this stage in my life, and that he'd be riding a white horse *and* flying his own plane.

I had *finally* received a kind twist of fate, just when I needed it most. Was Clint right? Had fate brought us together? I gave this new chapter of my life a lot of thought while Clint went on his ride.

Later we drove to the terminal and parked the jeep in a private parking space. No more jammed parking lots.

"This sure beats having to stand in a long line to check baggage, and then waiting in another long line to board a plane crowded with people and overstuffed with carry-on!"

We stood on the tarmac and admired the plane. "Come on, let's go." Clint opened my door. "Don't misconstrue my intentions," he laughed as he put his hand on my bottom and lifted me up to boost me in.

"Weather conditions look good," he said as he started the engines.

Nothing led us to expect that this would change during the flight. We flew over the ocean. For awhile, everything was fine and the flight went smoothly. Then the sky quickly turned dark.

"I think it's going to storm," I said, with no inkling of its ferocity.

"This is it. We're going to die." I shut my eyes and squeezed his hand. My mind went back to another time, and I recalled flying in a small Cessna as lightning struck the tail. I couldn't believe how charred it was when we landed. I was sure my lingering fear from that previous experience was written all over my face now.

"Relax," Clint urged. "Flying in a small plane is just as safe as flying in a big jet. Don't worry, everything will be just fine."

"I'll take your word for it. Still, it's pretty scary."

Somehow we made it to the Phoenix airport. I noticed that the sky looked kind of strange, the way it does before a tornado.

"I'd just as soon rent a car and drive the rest of the way," I said as I looked at the swirling clouds.

He laughed. "And you're an ex-stewardess?" Taking me by the hand, he led me to the car rental counter. We rented a Chevy Blazer equipped with four-wheel drive.

"Is this better?" he asked.

"Yes," I said doubtfully. In another gesture designed to make me comfortable, he reclined my seat.

"Just close your eyes."

"I think I will."

When I woke up after a short nap, I realized we were parked in the middle of a restaurant parking lot. I rubbed my eyes. "Where are we?"

"We're in Heber-Overgaard. I wanted to get past the worst mountainous curves before it got dark."

"Good idea. I'm glad I slept through that part."

"Are you hungry?"

"Yes." I looked out the window at the pouring rain. "Everybody for himself," I said as I opened the door and made a mad dash for the restaurant. Clint was already standing at the entrance holding the door open for me. The wind blew me right in.

"Not a very fancy place," he said.

"I know!" I laughed as I said it. "I've eaten here before. When my kids were young I used to bring them to Heber-Overgaard to participate in the Greased Pig Contest."

He just looked at me blankly.

"Fond memories." I smiled.

He scooted his chair next to mine. "Personally, I wouldn't care where we were, or what we were doing, just as long as I could be with you."

"That's nice of you to say."

"I thought so. Now, what would you like to order?"

"I'm going to pretend we're still in Mexico. I'll order the Mexican special and a cold beer with lime."

"Same for me," he said.

"Now that that's been settled, I'd like to freshen up."

When I returned, I saw Clint talking to a man seated at the next table. He turned toward me as I sat down. "This guy just came from the Four Corners Monument area. There are downed power lines all over the place. They've even closed parts of the road."

"Maybe we should abandon this idea," I said. "It seems like every time I pursue the *Chindi*, it storms. I've learned that when things are stacked against you, it's always better to wait. In my brother's case, I finally just gave up. I decided not to torture myself anymore. Instead, I wrote my book."

"Maybe so. But I don't like this bewitched element," he said in a rush of words. "There has to be a way to get rid of the curse. We can't quit now."

"I'll be free of the curse the day the killers are executed," I said.

As we got into the Blazer, I glanced in the mirror. "I look like a drowned rat."

"I like you just the way you are."

The rain was coming down in torrents. We drove to Holbrook, and then traveled east on Interstate 40 before turning onto a narrow reservation road that would connect us with the highway to Chinle.

I looked over at Clint as I snuggled down in my seat. "In hindsight, perhaps we should've taken the other route up north instead of the scenic route. It's too late to see anything, anyway."

"I don't think it would have made much difference. And the first opportunity I have, I'm going to pull over and stop."

Suddenly the Blazer lurched forward and slipped into a flooded wash. It bounced up and down a few times, and then crashed back down. Clint quickly shifted it into four-wheel drive, but it didn't move.

"Do you suppose somebody is trying to tell us something?"

After the storm passed, we waded out to assess the situation and the damage. By this time, it was almost dark.

While Clint was busy looking under the Blazer, I looked around. We were in the middle of a beautiful canyon. Something caught my eye. A wolf was standing on a ledge some twenty feet above me, its multicolored coat blending in with the unusual colors of the canyon wall.

"C-Clint," I stammered. "Look up."

The wolf didn't move.

"Jesus, why didn't you say something?"

"I just did! It looks an awful lot like Callista," I commented. "There are a lot of similarities. If it *is* Callista, it must be her spirit. When I last talked with the vet, he told me she was on the verge of death."

The wolf climbed down from the ledge and moved closer to where we were standing.

"She looks lonely."

"I wouldn't try to pet her."

She lifted her head and howled—a lone voice in the wilderness.

"I only wish I knew what she was saying."

Suddenly there was a surge of water as the damned-up area in the dry wash broke loose. It missed Clint, who was standing beside the Blazer, since he was smart enough to move away, but it knocked me over and pushed me downstream.

"Are you okay, Sarah?"

"Yes, I'm fine!" I yelled back as I sloshed my way to the bank after the wave crest had passed.

Clint moved quickly to where I was standing as it began to pour again. "So what's a few drops of rain?" He smiled. "At least the flash flood knocked the Blazer loose."

We waded out to it. "Nothing inside got wet," he said as he reached in and brought out a towel.

"I'm cold," I said as I snuggled up to him.

He wrapped the towel around me.

I looked around. The wolf was gone.

"Maybe that was my guardian angel. Nobody ever said you couldn't come back as a wolf."

"Or maybe it was your arch nemesis."

"You had to say that." I shivered.

We changed clothes quickly.

"Now that the storm is almost over, how would you like to spend the night under the starry skies?"

"Not on your life," I said. "Not with that wolf roaming around."

"We may have to. There may not be anything open when we get to Chinle."

"I'll take my chances."

It was very late when we arrived. We drove to the motel where I had previously stayed. It reminded me of the grim past. "If you don't mind, I'd prefer to stay somewhere else. The Thunderbird is just down the road."

Luckily, it was open.

I soaked in a tub of hot water. As it splashed over my shoulders, I stared at Clint as he stood in the open doorway, "A psychic once told me I had better watch my back."

"If you need someone to cover your back, I'm your man," he said seductively.

"I'm serious."

"I am, too."

He came and knelt before me. His arms went around my body and he hugged me tight. Stretching my hand up, I drew him closer, my heart beating hard against my chest.

"I would never let anything happen to you," he said.

I believed him.

The next morning, I put on several layers of clothing. The elevation on the reservation was six thousand feet. It would probably be a good idea to bring some rain gear, too.

"With some luck, we may even see a Kachina ceremony."

I packed my camera in my bag.

"Don't even think about bringing a camera to a Kachina ceremony. They'll confiscate it."

We headed out.

"Perched on top of six-hundred-feet-high mesas, the eleven villages of the Hopi Reservation offer two rare commodities: silence and tranquility," Clint explained. "The village of Old Oraibi on the Third Mesa may actually be the oldest continuously inhabited community in the United States. It's said to have been founded in the year 1050."

"Where does your friend live?"

"He lives on First Mesa, where there are three villages. His village is called Walpi."

"What is his name?"

"Redfeather."

As we drove, I couldn't help but admire the old adobe buildings, some of which dated back to the fifteenth century.

The Hopi priest greeted us warmly and introduced us to several members of his family, who were very kind to us. He politely asked me questions about what happened to my brother, and then shared his own insights.

"I wish I could tell you why this tragedy occurred or if it could have been prevented," he said. "There are no words to express my sympathy."

"The thing that makes it so hard is that my brother's death was so untimely." Thinking of it brought tears to my eyes.

"There's always a day of reckoning," Redfeather promised.

"I believe that good and evil actions in this life and previous lives affect the soul's rebirth."

"It's entirely possible."

I described my nightmarish experiences in more detail. "I could see and hear ghosts."

"The *Chindi*, as they are known in the Navajo culture, are trapped in spiritual bondage. They cannot pass on to the land of the dead. Any living thing can hold their spirit. From an Indian perspective, the name *Chindi* becomes a metaphor for evil. They will kill without mercy. In their eternal misery, they always come back. With very few exceptions, the only way to get rid of the curse is to send it back. But even that is not always foolproof."

Redfeather looked me squarely in the face. "Do you know who's responsible?"

"I believe I do, but I could be wrong."

"She knows," Clint interrupted us. "And I've done some checking on my own. Word on the street is your brother got involved in something that was none of his business. I figure drugs were part of the picture. He either knew too much, or was at the wrong place at the wrong time. Deputy Morgan seems to be a person of interest."

After two hours spent talking, Redfeather took me to a sacred location. There were stone ruins nearby. *It must have been a favored spot of the ancients,* I thought as I looked at the prayer circles scattered around.

I sat down on a stone wall under the shade of an old alligator juniper tree and watched him prepare for the ceremony. He was wearing an amulet, a small leather pouch decorated with sacred symbols.

"Native Americans use peyote as a sacrament, much like communion wine is used in Christian tradition. It contains the psychedelic drug mescaline. Drawn from the cactus button, peyote is eaten or ingested as a tea in ceremonies. A fire is kept burning, and the drumming and chanting last through the night. While large amounts can induce hallucinations, the small quantities normally taken in religious rites only produce an introspective mood that gives the user peace of mind and insight into the spiritual world."

He stared deep into my eyes. "Spiritually, you will be moved to take a deep look at your inner self."

It was a strange moment for me. There was a sense of peace and serenity, and also a little sadness.

"You must turn from the darkness," he said as the sun slipped below the horizon. "You must purify your soul. I will seek divine guidance for you."

The ceremony lasted from sundown to dawn. In many ways, it felt like an exorcism. The rite was essentially the same.

"Your brother's destiny has been fulfilled," Redfeather said as he revealed how my brother had suffered and died. "Now the murderers will know, and realize their destiny."

"I am thankful." I sighed deeply as I clutched his hand.

"May we all be wise enough to be thankful for the blessings we have."

Clint was waiting for me at the end of the stony footpath. "So, did you take it?"

I assumed that he was referring to the peyote.

"I'll never tell."

I buried my head in his shoulder. "I'm exhausted," I admitted. "I just hope the ritual worked. Redfeather told me it may be awhile before the results take effect."

"Now that it's over, how would you like to visit the Navajo Reservation? I have some distant relatives who would be more than happy to put us up for a day or so."

"Whatever we do, it had better not take much energy."

"Better yet, how would you like to spend the night in a traditional hogan? It may not have the luxury of running water or electricity, but it will acquaint you with the lifestyle of the Navajos."

"Oh, *that* sounds like fun," I quipped.

We drove for a short time. Upon entering the Navajo Nation, we stopped at a local gas station to ask for information.

"Do you happen to know the family of Victor Yazzie?" Clint asked.

Apparently the man did, but he answered in Navajo, so it was hard to tell.

"I hope you got all that."

"Most of it," Clint grinned.

Eventually we came to an isolated farmhouse. Off to the side was a traditional hogan. A man was standing outside, feeding some chickens. We got out of the car and Clint began speaking to him in Navajo.

"I wasn't sure if this was the right place," Clint said as he turned to me. "But it is, and we're invited to stay. This is my great-uncle George."

He introduced us.

"So, would you like to experience the life of a traditional Navajo sheepherder?" George asked me as he shook my hand.

"Just for a few days," I smiled.

"Follow me. Irene is making some mutton stew. Will you join us?"

"It would be our pleasure," Clint answered. "It's been a long time since I've had a traditional Navajo meal."

Throughout dinner, George and Clint carried on a conversation in the Navajo language. Occasionally, Irene translated for me.

"George suggested that tomorrow you could hike the canyons. He would be happy to be your guide."

"I'm game. How about you, Sarah?" Clint asked.

"I'll be ready when you are."

"That was a wonderful dinner," Clint said when we were through eating. "I hate to call it a night, but Sarah and I are exhausted."

"I understand," Irene smiled. "Would you like to use the bathroom or shower before you go to bed?"

"No, thanks. We already decided we wanted to have the privilege of sleeping on the floor and using the outhouse. We'll take some extra blankets, though."

"Shall I have George show you to your hogan?"

"No. it's okay. I saw it when we pulled in. We'll find it."

"I'm glad you at least took the extra blankets," I said once we were outside. We walked along the dirt path.

"Let me go in first and make sure there's nothing in there."

"Like what?" I asked.

He ignored me.

"All's clear," he yelled.

As I walked in, I could see his shadow in the light from the kerosene lamp. "You know, Clint," I said. "You're beginning to look more and more like an Indian." He already had his shirt off, and was standing barefoot in his jeans. "You have the physique of a young brave."

"Thank you," he said. "If you think I look like an Indian now, just wait until I let my hair grow long."

"I never know if you're kidding."

"You'll find out." He held me in his arms.

"Tonight you have the option of sleeping in the bed or on the same sheepskin that I slept on when I was growing up."

We were beyond exhausted after our episodic adventure as we collapsed on the floor. A romantic interlude was the furthest thing from both our minds.

The next day we hiked the canyons. It was tough, and I complained most of the way. But the trail crossed patches of greenery and areas where wildflowers proliferated along the narrow strip of canyon.

Most of the time, Uncle George scoured the ground for fossils. But not any old fossil. He was specifically looking for dinosaur fossils which, according to him, played an important role in origin stories.

After hours of hopping over rocks and climbing boulders, we finally stopped for lunch.

"Thank God," I sighed, trying to catch my breath.

Clint uncorked a bottle of wine and we sat down on the moist ground beside a trickling waterfall, sharing a turkey sandwich.

"Maybe you should consider writing a sequel to your book? Or perhaps turn it into a series," Clint said lazily.

"Maybe I will. Maybe our future is just waiting to be written."

After lunch, we resumed our hike. I turned to George. "I hope the pain in my lungs isn't quite so excruciating going downhill. Even the most experienced hikers would find these trails humbling."

He just laughed. That night we were invited to the wedding ceremony of Clint's cousin. I wore a special Indian costume borrowed from Irene.

"You look like an Indian princess," Clint beamed. "While you were with Irene, I dashed out and bought a gift for my cousin. It's a wedding vase. What do you think?"

It was beautiful. I realized he was not only good-looking; he had taste, too. So I told him so.

People were already gathered outside on the lawn. Just as the ceremony was about to begin, I remembered we had left our present—the wedding vase—back at the house. "I'll be right back, Clint," I whispered.

I wended my way back and searched the bedroom. There was no wedding vase. *Hmmm*, I thought, *I must have left it in the bathroom.*

As I walked down the hall, I heard a door close behind me. When I went to open it, it wouldn't budge. "That's strange. I never had a problem before," I mumbled to myself, turning the knob over and over.

I stood on my toes and looked out the window, but I couldn't see anybody. I realized it was probably too far to yell. Besides, I wouldn't want to interrupt the ceremony.

I managed to find a metal file in one of the drawers and used it to pry open the window. I removed the screen and carefully crawled through. *I hope I don't get Irene's dress dirty*, I thought as I made my way to the front of the house. It took me a while since it was already dark and difficult to see where I was going.

Suddenly, I stopped. There were two eyes watching me in a thicket of cedar bushes.

Oh, no!

I stood very still and listened to the quiet voice inside me. Slowly, I backed my way to the edge of the house. I felt a tiny bead of sweat trickle down my forehead. The eyes kept following me. When I got to the corner, I just ran. I made it as far as the back door, where I fell.

It was all too much. I gave up and screamed.

Clint must have heard me, because he promptly came running. "Are you okay?" he asked, picking me up off the ground.

"I guess so. Things like this just do not happen, especially to me. I've never had any confrontations with wildlife before."

Our gazes met, and I saw by his amused expression that he had somehow read my mind.

"Well, that's not entirely true." I paused, remembering the incident with the bear at the cabin. "The only time I've been stalked in the past was when I was trying to take a picture!"

Clint just laughed and carried me back to our hogan.

I slipped out of Irene's dress. All things considered, it didn't look too bad. "It's a shame that I missed the wedding ceremony," I said as I curled up on the bed. "Thank you for being here."

I closed my eyes and fell asleep.

The following morning, while we were having breakfast with Uncle George and Irene, we got a disturbing call from the airport. Somebody had broken into the plane.

"I'll bet that was no coincidence," I said to Clint when he was through talking. "The *Chindi* would like us to stay here. It's their territory. Maybe they have more power here."

Later that morning, we drove the Blazer to Flagstaff Pulliam Airport. Thankfully we were able to leave it at the Avis car rental agency. From there, we took a commuter flight to Phoenix. After we landed, we immediately went over to where the Piper Cherokee was parked. As far as we could see, other than the door that was ripped from the hinge, none of the other parts were disturbed or missing.

"Why would someone break in? What could their purpose have been?" I wondered out loud.

"I don't know. It seems suspicious, though. I just hope it wasn't an act of sabotage. Before we go back to the reservation, I'd like to test-fly the plane. I'll get a mechanic to fix the door and inspect the rest of it."

We spent the night in a motel. The next morning, we took the same shuttle bus back to the airport that had dropped us off the previous night. There was tension in the air. I could feel it.

"Are you nervous?" I asked.

"A little."

We boarded the plane. At first, Clint had some trouble closing his door. "I guess it's just stiff," he commented. "They probably replaced it with a new one."

He clicked on the control panel, and the dials and the gauges in the cockpit lit up. "So far, so good," he said.

Once we were in the air, everything seemed to go smoothly. We had our first spot of trouble when we were about fifteen minutes into the flight. Suddenly we felt a bump. The nose of the plane swung right, and the right wing dipped toward the ground.

Clint forcefully stepped on the left rudder pedal, but it was stuck. I looked at the ground. "Nothing's going to save us now," I gasped. I was convinced we were going to roll over. He turned the wheel to the left and added power to the right engine. The maneuver managed to bring the plane level. Then we heard the rudder release.

"Jesus," he exclaimed. "I've never had that happen before. Are you all right?"

"Yes," I said, my voice quivering.

"That was a close call!"

He banked the plane and turned back toward the airport. When we touched down, I was still so badly frightened that my knees were shaking.

"Maybe you need some grease in the rudder control system."

"I'm afraid it's worse than that. I suspect it was an act of sabotage. Perhaps this too is the work of the *Chindi*. All someone had to do was plant a tiny object with a spell attached to it. Even something like an insignificant piece of bone would do it. We don't notice it, and the plane goes down."

Could this be true? It sounded crazy, but maybe he was right.

"Oh, Clint," I said. "What are we going to do?"

"We're going to enlist a crew to take this plane apart, piece by piece, to make sure there's nothing in it that doesn't belong there."

"That could take days."

"Or longer. In the meantime, I'm going to check out Deputy Morgan, as I still think he had something to do with your brother's death."

"I don't see how that's going to help us."

"It may, especially if Morgan realizes we know that he and his buddies are responsible for the curse, and that we have the capability of returning it to them. They may back off, because whatever they've planned for us will happen to them instead. And I don't think they want that."

I waited in the airport while he made a few calls.

"There's no record to confirm that Morgan was ever at another trading post on the night of your brother's murder. His alibi won't wash. If we're able to find the article they planted on the plane, we could return it to them, along with the curse," Clint said with renewed enthusiasm.

"It sounds so simple, but so very diabolical. I just want to go back to Mexico."

"You can't escape this. You already know that. But, if that's what you want, we can go back."

Fortunately, we were able to catch a noon flight to Puerto Vallarta. After we landed, I looked over at Clint. "Before we go back to our hacienda, I'd like to stop at the vet's office and see how Callista is doing."

"We can do that," he said. "I'm just as anxious as you are to see how she's feeling."

"*Buenos dias*, Señor Walker and Señorita Simms," the vet greeted us. "You have good timing. Your little wolf just came back to this world."

"Is she okay?" I asked.

"Yes, she's doing fine. You can actually take her home now."

We loaded her into the jeep. She seemed happy to see us. After we arrived at Clint's residence, I called Callista over. She sat down next to me. "You certainly had a traumatic experience," I said as I petted her.

I noticed her eyes had a distant look. "Were you ever in Arizona?" I asked. She licked my hand.

"I thought so." I looked warmly at her. "You're my guardian angel."

That night, Callista slept at the foot of our bed. I had just fallen asleep when something woke me. I immediately sensed something was wrong, so I slipped out of bed and went over to where Callista was lying.

"I know you're hurting," I said, as I reached down to pet her.

She looked up at me and moaned. Suddenly her eyes changed color and took on an eerie, bright-red glow. Then the corner of her lips turned up in a snarl while white foam drooled from her mouth.

I snatched my hand back, but she snapped at me, catching her canine tooth on my hand.

"Oh, my God. What if she has rabies?"

She started to get up.

"Oh, no!" I screamed.

Clint jumped out of bed. "What's going on?" He turned on the light. "You scared me half to death."

"Take a look at Callista."

"I don't see anything wrong with her." Then he noticed the saliva dripping from the corner of her mouth. "We'd better get her to the vet, pronto. There's a muzzle somewhere in the storeroom. Do you think you can find it?"

"I'll try."

On my way there, I flipped on every light I could find. There was no telling what kind of creature might pop up from the mythical underworld. I had always been afraid of the unknown.

I searched the storeroom. Naturally, the muzzle was on the top shelf. Just as I reached for it, I heard a loud thud and a spine-shivering howl.

I ran back to the bedroom. Clint was holding a pewter urn with one hand and wrapping a towel around his arm with the other. "I had no choice," he said as he looked at Callista lying still on the floor. "She turned on me. I don't think she's dead, but she might as well be if she's got rabies."

Frantically, we transported her to the vet's office. We explained how she was acting and our fear of the possibility of rabies. He told us he would do a test right away and would have the results within twenty-four hours.

"You both realize that if she is rabid, we will have to put her down, right?" He suggested we go to the emergency room and have Clint's hand checked out.

The doctor on duty treated Clint's hand and took a look at mine. He prescribed us antibiotic cream to apply twice a day and urged us to keep the wounds clean. He also asked that we notify him of the test results from the vet. He said the test would probably come back negative and that we wouldn't need the painful rabies treatment shots.

We arrived home in the chilly hours just before dawn.

"I'm so scared," I confessed. "I doubt I'll ever be able to go back to sleep."

"Don't worry," Clint said as we lay down on the bed. "Everything will be fine."

"It's a comfort to know you're here beside me."

"I hope so," he said. "I'm glad I can be of some help."

Then neither of us fell asleep...Not for a long, satisfying time.

The next day, the vet called. We were surprised to learn that the test results came back negative.

"You mean Callista didn't have rabies?"

"That's right," the vet replied as I talked to him on the phone. "Thank God we didn't have to lose her. It could've been a reaction to the medication she was taking, or possibly a delayed reaction from her surgery, or both. If it isn't one of those things, I don't know what we're facing. She appears to be okay now."

What a relief! We brought her home later that same day.

"You don't suppose the *Chindi* invaded her body?" I remembered what the Hopi priest said. "Any living thing can hold their spirit."

"It sounds absurd, but the logic is perfectly sound. Finding the answers might be a lot easier if we knew what to expect."

The next morning, we got a call from the airport. It was from the crew chief who had been examining the plane. Just as Clint suspected, somebody had tried to sabotage it.

A tiny piece of bone pitted with tiny holes was found stuck behind the instrument panel. "Ordinarily, it wouldn't cause a problem, but it was positioned so that if it were to move slightly, it would short out the panel. It probably wouldn't have happened until you were in the air."

"They obviously weren't taking any chances," Clint fumed. "They wanted to make sure they had us in a double whammy. If I ever get my hands on that SOB, I'm going to ram my fist down his throat. Or worse."

Later that afternoon Clint flew to Phoenix and I stayed with Callista. That night, as Callista and I sat huddled by the fire, we had a long talk.

"You know about spirits, don't you? Of course you do. That was you on that ledge. There are good spirits and there are bad spirits. If anything evil tries to enter your body, you must resist it. And if you don't act fast enough, the two of us might not be here tomorrow to talk about it."

She seemed to know what I was saying.

I went through my jewelry pouch and found two dangling bear necklaces that were given to me as gifts. Which one should I wear? The one from the little Indian girl, or the one from Bobbie Jo?

One necklace was set with tiny beads of turquoise, the other in chunks of turquoise. I put one around my neck and looked at the other dangling bear necklace. Why not? I gently placed it over Callista's head. In Navajo mythology, the bear is the most powerful of beasts.

"That should protect you."

I was on the verge of falling asleep when Clint called.

"Is everything okay?" he asked.

"Yes," I said. "Although I have to admit, I'm not fond of the idea of staying here alone."

"I'll be back just as soon as I can."

The room grew cold when we hung up. Then the wind began to howl. *I hope that's the wind*, I thought as I got out of bed and put another log on the fire.

Suddenly the room began to fill with smoke. *Don't tell me the flue is stuck!* I thought about the time when I visited Clayton and he told me to make myself at home. He had neglected to tell me that I had to open the flue before I lit the fire.

This time the flue wouldn't move, so I opened the window instead. Then I ran to the adjoining bathroom, emptied a wastebasket and filled it with water.

As I stood with my back to the window dousing the fire, I heard a menacing growl. When I turned around, Callista was in an attack position, staring at the window. I was too afraid to go over and close it.

"Come, Callista," I called her. When I saw something withdraw into the shadows, I ducked behind a table. When everything looked clear, I ran out of the room, picked up the phone, and promptly called the police.

"I know you think I'm paranoid," I said to the officer as I stood there in my housecoat and slippers. "It's just that so many strange things have happened lately." I tried to explain further, but it only made me sound crazier, especially with the English-Spanish translations.

"I have a patrol car in the area," he said. "I'll try to reach the officer on the radio. If you see someone on the property, don't panic. It'll just be Officer Rodriquez."

"Thank you," I sighed in relief. "I appreciate your understanding."

It was almost noon before Clint arrived home.

"What's the police car doing parked in our driveway?" he asked.

"It's a long story..."

"There's nobody in the car."

"What do you mean?"

"Just what I said."

"Are you thinking what I'm thinking?"

We both panicked at the same time and ran outside.

"False alarm!" Clint said, as he observed the officer asleep on the patio lounge. "It can't be siesta time already!" Clint nudged him.

The officer didn't move. Then we realized the officer wasn't asleep; he was dead. "Call the police."

When the officer arrived, he made his way over to us.

"*Buenas tardes*, Señor Walkerman. We've been seeing a lot of each other lately. It appears that one of our officers keeled over and died of a sudden heart attack while patrolling your property. I don't suppose you know anything about it? People are dropping like flies around here."

Clint and I looked at each other. We both suspected it was another act of vengeance by the *Chindi*.

"It's about to come to an end. I think we got a lucky break." Clint smiled over at me as he held up a small object.

The officer looked at the tiny piece of bone. "I don't see how that's going to help us."

"It's an Indian thing."

"Whatever you say. I hope we don't see each other anytime soon. *Buenas tardes.*"

As the officer left, Clint turned toward me. "Now it's time for a little mean-spirited revenge." His eyes gleamed with a dark intrigue. "First, we'll target the ringleader. By reversing the curse, we're going to have to solicit the good spirits in order to protect ourselves from the evil powers of the *Chindi*. Then, they'll have a taste of what we've been enduring. Only this time, I'm going to invoke my own curse."

It sounded like an Indian "guy" thing to me.

"I don't know if I like the idea," I said. "There's a place in my heart that says it's not the right thing to do."

"For God's sake, Sarah! They killed your brother, and now they've come back to kill *you*!"

"It's one thing to return a curse; it's another thing to deliberately cast a spell on another human being with the intent to cause harm."

"Why the sudden benevolence?"

"I don't know. I'll never pardon them for what they've done, but maybe I just want to give them a chance to say they're sorry."

"Dream on! You don't have a ghost of a chance of that happening. Pardon the pun."

"Very funny."

"It's in our power to put an end to this nightmare right now, and that's exactly what we're going to do. I'll take care of everything."

Yeah, it was definitely a "guy" thing.

I sat down on the small Victorian bench on the patio. Clint sat down beside me and held my hand.

"I know you're searching for solace, Sarah, but I'm dealing with guilt on my side. I've asked myself so many times whether I could have done anything differently to prevent the murder of my wife. I've struggled with it for years, but now I realize I'm not to blame. And neither are you. It's about time we realize that we're not the ones who caused all this grief."

He rubbed my hand as he continued speaking.

"If it takes the rest of my life, I'm going to solve these murders. I've had my life threatened many, many times, but I don't like the idea of having *your* life threatened. There are some things worth fighting for, even dying for. And now I have to ask you a critical question."

He smiled as he looked deep into my eyes.

"There's something I need to know for my own peace of mind…Will you marry me?"

My head spun.

"Don't you think it's a little…early?" I gasped.

"Nonsense!" He picked me up in his arms and swung me around the room, kissing away my doubts.

"Yes, yes, yes!"

"I *knew* you were madly in love with me," he said.

"I can't wait to tell my kids that I've met an Indian cowboy who has swept me off my feet, and that I'm going to marry him! By the way, don't you have something else to tell me?"

"I love you."

That night we celebrated with champagne. The following day we flew to Sedona, Arizona, and were married in a simple ceremony. We spent the rest of the weekend at a romantic, secluded resort nestled in the red rocks of Boynton Canyon.

"I wish we could stay here forever," I said. "But I really need to get home and check on Mother and my animals. And, you know, inform my family that I'm now a married woman. You'll like Cornflower Corners. It's a cowboy town," I said matter-of-factly.

"Where is it?" he asked as he reached into his flight satchel and brought out his book of maps.

"There," I said, putting my finger on the page. "The streets do have names here," I said jokingly. "If only I could tell you what they are."

"Does it have an airstrip?"

"Sort of. The last time anyone tried to use it, they were unable to land because there were so many ruts in the runway. The alternative airport is Payson."

We flew back to Puerto Vallarta and unpacked and repacked our suitcases.

"Can we bring Callista back with us?" I pleaded. "I'm sure she'd rather be with us than stay here alone, especially now that Juanita is gone."

"I suppose it's better to take her with us than have to find someone who will watch her while we're gone, although my neighbors said they wouldn't mind. That is, until the gardener recovers."

"Has she ever flown in a small plane before?"

"No, but I'm sure she'll do fine."

We drove to the airport. While examining Callista, the vet had determined she was a hybrid, even though Clint had rescued her from a wolf's den. With the proper certificates and a clean bill of health, she passed easily through customs. We didn't have to ask twice if she wanted to go. She leaped on the plane.

"Wrangler is going to be so happy to see you." I playfully petted her. Then I whispered a confession. "I forgot to mention that Wrangler is from Alaska and that I suspect he's part wolf. He thinks he's the alpha male. He can be a little dominating."

"She'll adjust," Clint reassured me. "In the wolf pack, the key to getting along is reading social cues and doing what the dominant animal expects. Are you taking notes for yourself?" Clint laughed.

We landed in Phoenix. While Clint was refueling, I called ahead and made arrangements for someone to pick us up at the Payson airport. It made no sense for us to try to attempt a rough landing at the rural airport near Cornflower Corners.

My friend Mary Ellen, who worked for the Payson sheriff's office, picked us up as scheduled. After I introduced her to Clint, I told her the news.

"You got *married*?"

She was definitely in shock. Our wedding was going to be a big surprise to family and friends on both sides, most of whom were not aware that we even knew each other.

We drove straight to the house. It felt good to be home. I realized we would have two homes now—one in Cornflower Corners, and one in Puerto Vallarta. It didn't seem too bad at all.

We pulled up, and I saw Wrangler already waiting at the gate. He wagged his whole body as he greeted us. Then he sensed Callista's presence. What happened next totally surprised me. She walked over to him and boldly licked his face. There was no doubt about it: it was love at first sight.

We walked up to the deck, and there sat Mother having a cup of coffee. She had been left at home caring for my animals. "Well, if it isn't my long-lost daughter. I was beginning to wonder if you would be home before Thanksgiving. And who is that young man with you?"

I made a conscious effort to hold on to my self-possession. "In my own defense, Mother, I *have* called you often. This whole time, I have only been a phone call away. It's very good to see you."

I took Clint by the hand and took a deep breath. "Mother, I want you to meet Clint. I'm so glad you're sitting down for this, because Clint is my husband. We were married a few days ago in Sedona. I know this is sudden, but he really does make me very happy."

Mother stood up and gave Clint a regal hug, as if she welcomed new husbands into the family every day. "I'm glad to meet you, Clint. Now tell me, how did you convince my daughter to marry you? I never thought she'd marry again."

"Ma'am, your daughter and I were destined to meet and marry. I intend to take very good care of her."

Mother poured him a cup of coffee and told him to sit down and get acquainted. "Sarah, why don't you go and unpack before dinner?"

It was interrogation time.

Later that evening, Clint put his arm around me as we walked out onto the deck. Callista was lying with her paws draped over Wrangler's as they lay side-by-side. Mother had finished the dishes and gone home.

As darkness fell over the mountains, I cast my eyes toward the heavens. *I wish you could be here with us, Clayton. It doesn't seem fair.*

Suddenly I felt guilty about my newfound happiness. *You'll always have a special place in my heart*, I promised him as I fought back the tears.

Then I heard my brother's distant voice.

If it's any consolation, it isn't so bad here in heaven.

I couldn't believe what I was hearing.

Seriously, Sarah, please remember that in the end, love is the most important thing of all... Sometimes it felt like life moved much too fast. It wasn't easy to say good-bye, but it seemed as if Clayton was urging me to welcome another kind of love into my life. I turned toward my husband and hugged him gratefully.

Wrangler startled us both with a growl. "I think he's jealous," I laughed. "When I first moved to Cornflower Corners, I unwittingly became the beneficiary of two large dogs. They brought so much love into my life," I said as I thought about the circumstances that brought us all together.

"Sadly, the younger one died—tragically, I might add. For the last couple of months, I thought Wrangler was slowly dying from loneliness. Now with his new companion, his eyes are sparkling with life. I guess he just needed to put the past behind him. Like me, he's found it difficult to say good-bye."

Clint's fingers ruffled my hair comfortingly. "If you look, another door opens. With our memories, we never really have to say good-bye."

CHAPTER III

I had finally come to terms with my brother's death, but I still suffered with occasional flashbacks and unanswered questions. I wondered what his final words were before he took his last breath. Who had killed him? And why?

I sat by the edge of the creek next to my house, watching a leaf floating like a feather as it made its way downstream. I followed it with my eyes.

Suddenly I had another vision of my brother. I closed my eyes and tried to visualize what might have happened to him on that fateful night…

The snow had stopped falling, and Clayton had just arrived at the trading post. He and the person accompanying him stepped out of the truck onto the ice-crusted snow. They trudged up to the front door. Camille, the pretty Indian woman who was the last person to see my brother alive, was waiting inside the trading post.

"You can go now," Clayton told her. "Come pick up your check tomorrow. It should be ready by then."

She turned around and left for home.

Clayton went over to the refrigerator. "I'm starving," he said to the young man who appeared to be in his late teens or early twenties. "How about you?"

"Not really."

"You must be hungry. We haven't eaten all day."

Clayton reached into the freezer. He took out two steaks and set them on the kitchen counter along with some frozen corn to thaw. "When my nephews were about your age they had a ravenous appetite," he groused out loud.

"I'm just tired," the tall lanky man said. Then he walked out of the room.

But what had happened next? My mind always went blank when I reached this point.

"Sarah!" My husband roused me from my thoughts.

"What is it, Clint?"

"Look over there. Your little pet wolf just found a bone."

Callista was dragging part of a cow carcass. I noticed Wrangler, my big, black Labrador mix, was carrying a small stick.

"Apparently she doesn't want to share her new treasure."

"That's just like a woman," Clint laughed.

"Don't be so chauvinistic!"

"Seriously, I wish you'd confide in me what you're thinking. Perhaps I can help?"

"Okay. Every once in a while I get this vision, but just as I reach the critical part where I'm able to visualize what happened to my brother, a veil drops in front of my eyes and clouds my mind."

"You need to go back to the trading post where it happened," Clint said. "I'd be glad to go with you. We can take Callista and Wrangler with us for added protection."

"I'm sure there won't be any clues after all this time."

"The spirits have the answers, and time doesn't affect spirits. Between your psychic ability and mine, the pieces of the puzzle just might come together."

"That would be wonderful. When do we leave?"

"The sooner the better. There's no telling when the weather will turn bitterly cold. Even leaving now we're taking a chance. Just last week my friend in Springerville told me there wasn't an acorn or a nut left on the ground. That tells me it's going to be a long, hard winter. Do you suppose the animals know more than we do?"

"I'm concerned about the weather, too," I admitted as we got ready to leave. "I hope we don't get snowbound. Do you think we'll have to spend the night?"

"Absolutely."

"Not at the trading post, I hope?"

"Yes."

"But you don't know what that's going to be like!"

I remembered my first trip to the trading post when I had heard those hideous voices screaming out of the dark. It was the same thing during a return trip with my friends.

"Besides, the place has been trashed. There's no place to sleep."

"Then you'd better pack your sleeping bag. Unless you'd rather sleep with me in mine?" He smiled.

"Oh, Clint, I really don't know if I could spend the night in that creepy place."

"Let's see how it goes. It might not be as bad as you think," Clint encouraged. "Unfortunately, we'll have to take your truck, since our new jeep hasn't arrived yet."

"Mother is not going to be happy with us leaving before the holiday."

"We should be back in time for Thanksgiving. You better go tell her."

I was right; she was very disappointed. After the long drive, we stood outside the trading post.

"It's even worse than I thought," I said.

I noticed the windows were all boarded up; what I *didn't* notice were the three men who were hiding in the bushes behind us.

We approached the main door. The dogs eyed it warily, having returned from following a scent.

"You go in first," I commanded. "Who knows what's crawling around in there."

"There's more to worry about than rattlesnakes and scorpions," Clint remarked. "I see fresh tracks all over this place. And they're not all human tracks," he added as he pushed the sand with his shoes. "This one was made by a bear."

"This bright idea of ours really needed more thought," I mumbled loud enough for Clint to hear.

Just then, three men armed with rifles surrounded us.

"What are you doing here?" one of them asked.

Another man, his head wrapped in a red checkered scarf, suggestively fingered the trigger on his gun.

"This is private property," the first man said.

The third man, dressed in a black leather jacket, held an AK-47 rifle to Clint's head. "Are you a narc?" he asked.

"No way," Clint answered.

"I'm sorry," I intervened. "This is all my fault. We were just exploring. I didn't realize it was private land."

The man with the itchy trigger finger stared at me. "I know you. You're the lady who was nosing around here last year. You're Clayton Conway's sister."

"Is that so?" The third man reached down and pulled the Colt .45 from Clint's holster. "And I suppose you're her private body guard."

The man then pushed us through the doorway and whacked Clint's head with the butt of his rifle. The dogs barked excitedly, still puzzled by all the activity.

"Stay," I commanded.

Callista stared at Clint, but Wrangler sensed my fear. He dove over a chair and barreled full-force into the man, knocking him over. A scuffle broke out. Clint was able to retrieve his gun, but not for long.

One man kicked the gun out of his hand and the man in the red scarf began beating him. Callista and Wrangler hurled themselves at the assailants, stabbing at them with their teeth. By then, the man in the black leather jacket was on his feet. He pointed his gun at Wrangler.

"No!" I screamed, running toward the man who was holding the gun. But it was too late; he obviously had no qualms about shooting a dog.

The man grabbed me. "You'd better call off that other mutt, too, unless you want me to put a bullet in her as well."

The crack of the rifle sent Callista scurrying through the open door.

"Run!" I called after her.

Clint was lying on the floor bleeding, semiconscious.

"Get rid of these two troublemakers," the third man instructed the other two. "Lock them in the walk-in safe room. It's big enough, and they'll never get out of there."

The two men dragged Clint across the dirt-streaked cement floor and into the safe. I followed, a gun nudging my back. The third man said something in Navajo. Then he grabbed me and pushed me into the room. I landed on top of Clint as the door bolted behind me.

"Oh, sweetheart," I cried softly. "Are you okay?"

"Yes," Clint said. "I may have hit the nail on the head when I suspected drugs were involved. The man who spoke Navajo indicated that a shipment of cocaine was due in later today."

"No wonder they don't want us around." Tears sprang to my eyes and I clung to my husband. "My poor, poor Wrangler!"

"I don't think he's dead. As they were dragging me away, I noticed he was still breathing a little."

"I hope he survives. God bless him," I prayed. "What do we do now?"

"I don't know yet."

I looked around. "This is the room where the spirits' voices emanated."

"The spirits are the least of our worries!" Clint exclaimed.

Then I heard a horrible noise. I nudged Clint for confirmation.

"Yes, I heard it."

It sounded as if the spirits were coming through the floorboards. I huddled in the dark corner, shivering.

Clint got out his lighter. "There's a deep crack in the floor," he said as he ran his fingers over it, brushing off the dust as he traced its course.

"It makes a complete circle. I wonder if this could be the floor safe that Clayton installed?"

We heard a scratching sound.

"You hold the lighter," Clint said as he fumbled for his knife. "I'm going to pry this open."

After a few minutes, he reached under the rim of the lid with his two fingers and lifted it. Something huge leaped from the deep hole. I dropped the lighter and yelped.

Clint grabbed me and put his hand over my mouth. "It's Callista!"

"Oh, my God! I am so happy to see you!" I scratched the soft fluffy fur on her neck. "I'll never complain about your digging again."

"I wonder how she got in here," Clint said as he climbed down into the opening. "This appears to be a tunnel. Let's find out where it goes. You can lead," he said as he petted Callista's head. "You have better night vision."

We scrambled down into the hole. The tunnel was so narrow we had to crawl on our bellies. It felt very claustrophobic. As we followed the tunnel, it led us to a huge cave.

"I always wanted to be a cave spelunker," Clint quipped.

"You remind me of my brother. I thought he was the only person who could turn a grim situation into a joke."

I recalled a time when I was hiking with my sons. Clayton had agreed to meet us at a specified time and place with our lunch; naturally, he wasn't punctual. Four hours later he showed up. "Well, if it isn't the 'happy hikers!"

he'd exclaimed when he saw the dour expressions on our faces. I had to laugh at the memory.

"I wish I could have met him. I know I would've liked him, especially if I remind you of him."

The cave had several cracks and fissures that allowed some light to filter in. "Look at these mysterious inscriptions on the wall."

"Those are Anasazi hieroglyphics. This is probably where they did most of their cooking." I glanced up at the ceiling, just as Clint had done. The ledge above us was blackened and streaked from smoke.

"It won't be long before it gets dark," he warned. "I think we'd better get situated for the night. They must've had some sleeping chambers somewhere in this labyrinth of rooms."

"Shouldn't we keep going? What if those thugs notice we're missing? What if they decide to come after us?"

"I doubt if they know about this cave. If they did, they wouldn't have put us in that room."

"True."

I climbed down onto another ledge. The cave grew darker and colder. "Where are you, Clint?"

I reached for his hand, but he didn't answer.

"Clint! Don't be funny!" I said in the steeliest voice I could muster.

Suddenly I heard Callista growl; then she began to whine.

"What is it, Callista?" I said as I took another step. Suddenly I felt something cold and wet at my feet.

"Guess who's here?" Clint called out. "It's Wrangler."

"My God! I can't believe it. Where are you?"

"We're across the river."

"What river?"

"The one you're probably standing in. Stay there. We'll be right over."

"I couldn't make up a story like this if I tried," I sighed.

Clint finally found me. I felt the warm muzzle of Wrangler's nose as he stood beside me.

"When I heard his panting, I wasn't sure if it was a wild animal or what. I took my gun out of my boot just in case," he said.

"You managed to keep a gun?"

"Yes, it's a Ruger .357 caliber."

"That's a promising sign. We might get out of this place alive yet!"

Clint took me by the hand. "Let's go back up to where there's some light. At least now we know where to find water."

"Now that I think about it, Clayton once told me he found an underground cave with a subterranean river running through it. According to him, it went on for miles. The water was so black and dark that the fish living in the river had no eyes. They had no need for them. I'm still amazed at the evolutionary process."

"That's interesting. Now I know where to find dinner!"

We started up to the main part of the cave and the dogs followed. As we got to the top, I noticed Wrangler was staggering. "Poor baby," I hugged him. "If we ever get out of here, I'm going to give you the biggest bone I can find. Even bigger than the one Callista found that day at the creek."

"I'm sure he understands."

"He does."

"Here, boy!" Clint said as we sat down on the rocks. "Let me look at your wound. It doesn't look too serious. The bullet just grazed his skull. It probably stunned him more than anything."

"Don't minimize what he went through. He tried to save our lives!"

"I realize that." Clint smiled warmly at Wrangler. "Okay. First thing when we get home, I'll give you a big bone, too."

"I wonder how Wrangler found us?"

"He probably discovered the hole that Callista made when she dug her way into the tunnel. Smart dog!"

Within a few minutes, the cave grew dark. It was as if someone had turned out the lights. "I guess this is where we're sleeping tonight," Clint said.

"I'm cold," I complained. "Not only that, my feet are wet."

"What do you want me to do about it? Oh, all right," he grumbled. "You can have my socks."

"Thanks." I snuggled up to him.

"Now what's my treat?" he asked.

"You'll get your treat when we get home."

"Can I have a sample now?" He began to unbutton my shirt.

"Not in front of the dogs," I laughed.

For the remainder of the night, I slept with my head on Clint's shoulder. At one point I felt cold wet drops hitting my chest. *It must be my imagination. Perhaps it's just condensation,* I convinced myself.

When I woke up the next morning, Clint was leaning over me.

"I don't want you to panic," he said sternly.

"What is it?" I asked as I started to get up. I glanced down at my sweater. It was covered with blood. "Oh, my God!"

"Don't be alarmed. It's probably from an injured animal that crawled into the cave to die."

"Maybe it's still alive."

"Looking at all this blood, I doubt it."

Clint helped me up. The dogs rallied around me. They probably thought *I* was injured.

"Let's go down to the river. We can check out the upper chamber later."

"My, this water's cold!" I shivered as I stood naked at the edge of the river. Leaning over a rock, I carefully rinsed my sweater. Something brushed my hand. I could only imagine what it was, so I pulled back my hand, wrung out my sweater, and placed it over a rock to dry.

"Come on, get in." Clint's voice rose from the darkness.

"No, *thank you*," I replied. "It's one thing getting my feet wet standing here naked, but believe me, there's no way I'm getting in this icy water. Besides, who knows what kind of prehistoric monsters are swimming around in here? I'll just stay on the edge and bathe."

That's the quickest bath I've ever taken, I thought as I finished dressing. Clint was still splashing around in the water and so were the dogs. "Hurry up!" I called out. "We're not vacationing at a spa!"

One of the dogs came up and shook water all over me. "I wasn't talking to *you*."

My stomach rumbled. "I wish we had some food," I complained.

"There are all kinds of fish in here," Clint said. "Too bad I'm a modern Indian. My ancestors would have just jumped in and grabbed one."

"Have Wrangler help you. He knows how to catch fish," I said smugly.

"Go get a fish, Wrangler!" I commanded.

He went over to the edge of the river and soon came back with a fish flapping in his mouth.

Clint came up behind me. "If you're not careful, you could easily slip into that frigid water." He put his hands on my shoulders. "Do you think *you* could catch a fish?"

"Behave yourself," I said, pushing him away. "This is no time for fooling around."

We climbed back up to the grand room of the cave.

"Let's go this way," Clint directed as we squeezed through a narrow passageway that led upward. I felt more shivers as we began to explore the cave.

"I'd like to find that dead animal. It may have to suffice for dinner. In fact, it may mean the difference in our survival."

"Are you serious?"

"Yes."

"I think I just lost my appetite."

As we climbed up several tiers onto another level, Clint peered through the rocks. "We should be just above our sleeping quarters now."

He took the gun out of his boot. "Stay behind me, and hang on to those dogs. If there's a bear in here, or even a den of bears, which is what I suspect from the claw marks on the wall, the sound and scent of the dogs will only rouse their curiosity or aggravate them."

As we rounded a curve, Clint pointed his gun. "It's a bear. Thankfully it appears to be dead."

"Phew," I sighed.

"Keep the dogs back until I make sure."

"Easier said than done. I'm pretty sure they've never seen a bear before."

He followed the blood-soaked footprints to a large brown animal. It appeared to be in a peaceful, hibernation-like state.

"It's okay. You can release them."

Instead of running toward the bear, the dogs leaped onto an upper ledge and began running down another passageway.

"I wonder what prompted that?"

Clint grabbed me by the hand and pulled me up onto the ledge. "If you don't mind, I'll go on ahead. You can catch up to me at your own pace."

"Gladly. But what if I get lost?"

I started to make my way through the cavern. All the while, I had a creepy feeling that someone or something was following me. I picked up the pace. Then I heard it. There was no mistaking it: it was definitely the voice of the *Chindi*.

I stopped dead in my tracks. The sounds became louder. *It'll be a miracle if we ever get out of here alive.*

I noticed a small indentation in the rocks and quickly crawled into it, huddling in the corner. As the piercing howls continued, I sat with my hands cupped over my ears.

What was it trying to tell me? What was it trying to say? The last time I had heard those spine-shivering sounds it had been a warning...to get out. I wished I could.

Then the voices stopped. I jumped out of my hiding place and started running.

"I never knew I could run so fast!" I exclaimed breathlessly as I caught up to Clint.

"I'm so glad you're okay." He held out his arms. "I was just on my way back to find you."

"Did you hear those sounds?"

"It was impossible not to. Weirdest noises I've ever heard. And I thought we had problems *before*! I still haven't been able to find the dogs. Would you rather rest for a bit or continue?"

"I'd like to get out of here as fast as we can."

"Me, too."

In the distance, we could hear the dogs barking, so we followed the muddy footpath in the direction of the sound. When we caught up to them they were barking at something in the corner of the cave. But what?

Then I saw a poor, pathetic-looking creature crumple to the floor with a whine.

I immediately called the dogs to me.

CHAPTER IV

"Good grief!" I gasped. "It's a little boy!"

He scrambled up and began to run.

"Don't!" I yelled out.

He stuttered to a stop.

"We're not going to hurt you," I reassured him. "We're just as afraid as you are."

He turned around and looked at us suspiciously.

"*Now* what do we do?"

I looked at Clint for support.

"I don't know, but I don't blame him for being afraid," he answered.

We stared at the boy. He seemed roughly ten years old, with dark brown eyes and dark skin. From his disheveled appearance, he looked as though he had been living in this cave for years.

"Do you think he's Navajo?"

"He looks more Hispanic than Indian."

Clint said something to him in Spanish.

"*Sí,*" the boy replied.

"You're making progress."

"What would a kid be doing all alone in a cave?"

"Ask him where his parents are."

"They're dead, *estan muertos*," the boy said sadly.

He approached us tentatively. When I held out my arms, he almost flew into them. I hugged him tightly. He was shivering.

"Everything's going to be okay," I whispered.

I led him to a cluster of rocks. As we sat down, the dogs went up to him and licked his face.

"It could use a good cleaning," I smiled. He seemed to know what I was saying.

As the temperature in the cave began to drop, I realized we hadn't eaten all day. "I'm hungry," I said.

The boy jumped up. He said something to Clint in Spanish.

"He says he has some food stashed away in a secret tunnel. Lead the way," Clint told him.

The boy led us further down the passageway. When we came to a dead end, he suddenly stopped. There was a boulder blocking what appeared to be another passageway. He slithered his way behind the boulder and motioned for us to do the same.

"I don't think so," I muttered, knowing full well that there was no way I could get my hips through that opening.

"Help me move the boulder," Clint said. As we pulled and tugged, the boy pushed. Finally, we were able to move it.

As we ducked inside the entrance, it opened to reveal a huge cathedral-like cavern. It was truly *awesome*.

"I wonder how long he's been living here," I said.

He had accumulated all sorts of things: pottery, cans, crude weapons, and even some sort of a tarp that he had made into a makeshift tent.

"Quite the little homemaker," I smiled.

"I'll say. Look over here."

There was a fire pit in the middle of the room. Lying next to it was a pile of dead fish.

"Sushi, anyone?" Clint said.

"That's amazing. How did you learn to catch fish?" I asked the boy.

Clint repeated my question in Spanish.

"He says that his papa taught him before he died."

After we officially introduced ourselves, Clint sat down and talked further with the boy. He discovered that his name was Pablo, and that he could speak a little English. He'd had a mother, a father, and a sister, all of whom were dead.

"How did it happen?" I asked quietly.

"Coyotes," Clint answered.

"They were killed by prairie wolves?" I asked incredulously.

"No, silly. They were immigrants being transported illegally by smugglers referred to as Coyotes."

"Oh, I see," I said, embarrassed.

I turned to Pablo. "I'm glad you know some English, because I know very little Spanish. I took French when I was in school. A lot of good that did me!"

Pablo began to laugh. "I learned some English from the nuns who came to our village."

"It's good to see there is a handsome smile under that crop of hair," I smiled at him.

"Poor little guy," I said as I looked over at Clint. I wondered when he had last felt the warmth of a real home.

"I'm sure he's been through a lot. I have a hunch that if we can find out who he is, or even something about his background, part of our mystery might be solved."

Pablo pulled a photograph out of his baggy jeans and showed it to us. There were two people in the picture; a man in his late thirties with wavy black hair, and a pretty, petite woman. It looked as if they were working in a cornfield.

"Is that your mama and papa?"

"Yes. They came to Arizona to find work. But instead, all they found were their graves. Not even proper graves," he added dejectedly.

"What do you mean?"

He picked up a silver and turquoise cross.

"That's a beautiful piece of artwork. Where did you find it?"

"It was my mother's cross."

"Where is she?"

"Out on the hillside with the others who were killed."

"How did you escape?"

"I ran away and hid in this cave."

"Why didn't you leave?"

"I was too afraid. Besides, where would I go?"

"Where are you from?" I inquired gently.

Pablo lowered his head. "Juárez. I come from a poor family of farmers."

"So you and your family were smuggled across the border to find work?"

"Yes. We were loaded into a van without knowing where they would take us."

"Keep in mind," Clint said as he looked over at me, "Juárez is a major distribution center for the illegal drug traffic between the United States and Mexico. The Juárez Cartel has a reputation for being one of Mexico's bloodiest during turf wars along the Chihuahuan border for control of the lucrative South American cocaine trade."

"I take it lots of people have mysteriously disappeared after crossing the border."

Pablo turned to me. "Were they kidnapped and killed like my family?"

"Yes," Clint answered.

"How many?" I asked.

"It could be hundreds, but more likely it's thousands."

"I thought I had closed the worst chapters in my life, and now you tell me *this*?"

"Do you have a pencil and some paper?" Clint asked Pablo. "Sarah is a book writer. She's written a novel about her brother's murder. She plans to write lots of books about killing…and drugs."

"What?" I asked, astonished.

"Books," Pablo said. "*Libros.*"

"The plot thickens," Clint continued with a gleam in his eyes. "There may even be a subplot developing in the shadows. It appears we're not only dealing with drug traffickers, but with an international smuggling ring as well."

Pablo disappeared for a few minutes. When he returned, he was carrying a small blue notepad. He handed it to me, along with a worn down pencil.

"That'll do," I said as I began jotting down some notes.

"Can you show us where you found the cross?" I inquired.

"Yes, but it's dangerous. There are three men who sometimes patrol the property."

"We've already met them," Clint grimaced. "One of them knocked me around."

Pablo gave him a startled look. "I'm surprised you're alive! They're the ones who shot the mama bear. And now the papa bear is all alone," he added.

"There's a papa bear?" I gulped.

"Yes. They shot at him, too, but they missed."

"How could they miss a target that large?"

"Before they had a chance to lift their guns, the bear backed them up to the edge of a deep gully. They lost their balance and fell."

"You're not making this up, are you Pablo?"

"No," he answered, confused.

"I presume the bear you're talking about lives in this cave."

"Yes."

Suddenly we heard a grunting sound and then a huge roar. Pablo seemed undisturbed by the fact that a raging bear might be sharing his premises.

"Don't worry. So far the bear hasn't figured out how to move that boulder."

I looked at Pablo in concern. "Please tell me that you and Clint remembered to put that boulder back in place?"

"We did."

"Well, that's comforting at least!"

"Okay, son. Where's all this food you told us about?" Clint interrupted.

"Wait right here." Pablo stepped into the back of his secret cubbyhole that was hidden in a tiny nook in the cave. He emerged seconds later carrying beef jerky and a large basket of *piñon* nuts.

"Feast your eyes on this!" I said, delighted. "All we need now is a bottle of wine."

"Your wish is my command, señora."

Pablo handed me a can filled with some crushed, cherry-red berry juice. Then he poured one for himself.

"Would you like one too, Señor Clint?" He stood smiling in his threadbare tee shirt, waiting for a response.

"Why not?" Clint winked at me.

"The dogs should have enough to eat, too," Pablo said as he threw them each a large meaty bone left over from a cow carcass he'd found outside.

We spent most of the night talking and drinking the diluted berry juice. It was after midnight when we finally decided to call it a night. I dropped off immediately and fell into a deep, dreamless sleep.

It was very early when the bats came. Hundreds of them flew into the cave just before dawn.

"Why didn't you warn me about them?" I chastised Pablo. One of them swooped down and fluttered against my cheek, but this time I didn't flinch.

What was it with bats and me? I always seem to encounter them. I closed my eyes and somehow managed to go back to sleep.

I woke up again much later, this time with the worst hangover of my life.

"What did you put in that juice?" I asked Pablo, who was already up and about.

"Tequila."

"Where did you find *that*?"

"In the trash pile, along with the dead bodies."

"Good God! Glad I asked!"

"Come, señora. If we don't go now, we won't make it to the gravesite until dark. It's a long journey."

"I don't know if I want to go see the bodies. I've seen enough tragedy already."

"Oh, please, señora! You and Clint might be able to find out who murdered all those people. There isn't a day that goes by that I don't think about my family."

What could I say? I knew exactly how he felt.

"Okay. Give me a few minutes. At least let me wash my face. And you'd better do the same."

Both dogs were curled up on a blanket, nose to tail. "Time to get up," I announced. Callista went prancing off after something she smelled in the dark. Wrangler needed a little more coaxing.

"Come on, big boy," I coddled him. Within seconds he was off looking for Callista. I didn't worry about them. Both dogs had spent a lot of time living by their wits.

"You can always tell how a person treats people by how they treat animals," Pablo observed.

"Very astute," I praised him. "Smart," I corrected myself, remembering that English was his second language.

"Why do you call her Callista?"

"One of Jupiter's moons is named Callisto. Since Callista is part wolf and loves to howl at the moon, Clint named her Callista. Wrangler is also a wild dog and part Labrador retriever."

Pablo's brown eyes grew large. "Wow! How did you tame them?"

"With love and discipline. The same way you do with kids. Although, I must admit, I can't take all the credit. Clint trained Callista."

It was too early to take notes, but I wanted to be prepared. I stuck the blue notepad and the worn-down pencil into my pocket.

"Are you ready?" I asked.

Clint squeezed my hand. "As ready as I'll ever be."

"Let's go." I grimaced as I pondered our uncertain future.

"You know, we'll never beat the war on drugs," Clint said as he grabbed his gun.

"I know. But we can do *something*. I just hope they don't retaliate."

"What do you mean?" Pablo inquired.

"It wasn't too long ago that someone got even with me by killing my other dog, Roper."

"*Bastardos!*"

"I wholeheartedly agree. But if we waste our energy hating, evil wins. Now Callista has a good home and is part of our family. She will never take the place of Roper, but she is just as important to me."

"She's important to me, too," Pablo said as he watched her tail wag. "I think she knows we're talking about her."

"She does. Are you ready?" I asked.

I had no sooner said the words than Callista jumped up on me. "Okay, girl! You go ahead and scout the trail. We'll be along soon."

The dogs took off, eliciting gales of laughter from Pablo, who found delight in chasing them.

"Shall we go?"

Clint picked up the flashlight Pablo had given him. I tried to wipe the dirty paw prints from my shirt.

"I'm still trying to get over the notion that clothes should be clean."

After what seemed like hours of tromping through deep dark tunnels, our lengthy struggle to survive began. At one point, I fell while wading across the underground river and was swept a few yards away in the frigid water.

Completely desperate, my clothes wet, and my legs stiff, I put my head in my hands and just cried. Clint came over to make sure I was okay. "I'm so cold I hurt," I said.

"Think about warm things. Mind over matter," he urged, giving me his jacket. Eventually he broke down and lit a fire, a mistake that nearly cost us our lives.

We had just started to relax when, out of nowhere, we heard the bear prowling, clacking its jaw, and growling ominously. The two dogs raced toward the shadows and lunged as if attempting to attack the bear. That gave us some time to move farther away. I didn't see Pablo the entire time, which worried me.

"That took at least ten years off my life," I sighed. "I think I actually look my age now."

"You look beautiful." Clint kissed me. "Let's go find Pablo."

We didn't have far to look. He was cowered in a little ball in a nook in the cave.

"Your dogs frightened that bear," Pablo said excitedly as he hugged us.

Clint whistled for them, and they immediately came bounding in our direction.

"Thankfully they're not hurt!" I exclaimed when I saw their happy faces. "Good, brave dogs!"

We all sat huddled together by the fire.

"Why don't you take your pants off and put them by the fire to dry?" Clint asked.

"Why don't you take *your* pants off?" I taunted.

"I don't want to be caught with my pants down."

"One of us has to be daring," I said as I squirmed out of my jeans. "At least your jacket is extra-long."

I turned to Pablo. "How much farther do we have to go?"

"I'm not sure if we should go any farther," he admitted. "I'm afraid."

"How can a boy who lives in almost total darkness be afraid of anything?"

"I'm not afraid for myself. I'm afraid for you."

"Oh, sweetheart," I hugged him. "Don't worry. I have two guardian angels that always protect me." I nodded toward Wrangler and Callista. "I'm sure they'll protect you, too."

I took out my pencil and sighed. "Nobody is going to believe this. They'll think I've fabricated events that never took place."

"I think most novels are a mixture of truth and fiction," Clint said, "and I'll bet the writers don't know which is which! It wouldn't surprise me if Lewis Carroll truly believed that Alice crashed the Mad Hatter's Tea Party," he teased. "It's too dark to write now, though. Come on. We have to find a safe place to hole up. That bear may come back."

We waited just long enough for my pants to dry.

"We should be there soon," Pablo volunteered.

For the next half hour or so, we inched our way upward, climbing over one basketball-size boulder after another. Finally, we came upon a flat landing.

"I have to rest for awhile." My breath whistled. *Why hadn't I spent more time running with the dogs instead of driving while they ran?*

"Not again?" Pablo grunted.

"Yes, again! This is not an *Indiana Jones* movie. This is *real!*"

We sat down on the dirt and I turned to Pablo. "How long have you been climbing around in these tunnels?"

"I'm not sure," he said. "There has been only one snowfall."

"That's a convenient way to measure time, especially in a situation like this. Speaking of time, I wonder what day it is?"

Clint looked at his watch. "It's Thursday."

"Today must be Thanksgiving! Usually I'd be up at dawn, chopping onions and stuffing the turkey before breakfast. And I bet Mother is champing at the bit because we're not there."

"Do you have a big family?" Pablo asked.

"It's a rather small family, actually," I answered.

I pictured my loved ones gathered around the dining room table: my mother, my two sons and their wives, my grandchildren, Clint and me, and the empty place where my brother once sat.

"We had better keep going," Clint said, sensing that I was becoming nostalgic. Still, there was a soft side to this man. He came over and put his arm around my shoulders.

"I can't imagine life without you, Clint," I whispered softly. "I love you."

"I love you, too. If only you knew how much."

"Please tell me. You know I never get tired of hearing you profess your endless love."

"Enough mush, darling. Let's go!"

"Do you think our lives will ever return to normal?" I sputtered as I tripped over a rock.

"I thought you *liked* a challenge."

"I do," I grumbled, "although I don't remember telling you that."

I got to my feet and pressed forward.

"Are you two fighting?" Pablo wanted to know.

"Of course not. That's just love talk," I said.

In order to make up for lost time, we decided to take a shortcut.

"We're almost there," Pablo said.

Finally, I spotted a glimmer of light ahead.

"Do you see what I see?" I asked in a singsong voice. "Tell me it's not a mirage."

"It's not a mirage, but it's not the end of our journey, either."

As we approached the opening, Pablo looked at Clint. "I don't get it!" he exclaimed.

"What don't you get?"

"This entrance, it's always boarded up. I always have to take a board off to crawl through. There must be something going on."

We could see a few people coming and going. Then we spotted the man in the black leather jacket. As he stood there, his gun slung over his shoulder, he reminded me of some sort of rebel warlord.

Our first problem arose when Wrangler barked.

"Quiet!" I grabbed him.

The man in the black leather jacket poked his head in the opening.

"Get down!" Clint whispered.

I crouched down and held my breath. Suddenly the room exploded in a burst of gunfire.

"Stay down!" Clint instructed. "*Everybody*! That means you, too," he glared at Callista and Wrangler, who were both ready to attack.

After the firing stopped, I looked over at Clint. Surely that heavy breathing wasn't coming from him? I glanced behind me.

"No!" I cried in disbelief. As I stared into the red, fiery eyes of the bear, it ran past us, charging toward the cave's entrance.

We wouldn't find out until later what happened after that. From what we could see, the bear was advancing toward the man in the black leather jacket. All we heard was gut-wrenching screams, and then silence.

I crawled over to Clint. "Do you suppose it's safe to venture outside?" I was dreading what we might find.

"I don't know. I don't hear anything, but I don't know what to expect." Clint stood up slowly. "You and Pablo stay here for a few minutes. I'll take the dogs with me and see if I can find out what happened."

Moments later, they all returned.

"I'm glad to see you're still in one piece!"

"Nobody else is, unfortunately. There are body parts strewn all over the place. It's not a pretty picture. Aside from that, though, it's snowing!"

"I can't imagine why you're so excited," I said. "Now we're going to freeze to death!"

"Not in the cave, we won't. It stays at a pretty even temperature in there. Besides, I'm not worried. I have my love to keep me warm."

We held each other's hands as we walked out of the cave. I looked up at the white wintry sky, as the fresh flakes of snow fell onto my face. "We actually do have a lot to be thankful for on this Thanksgiving Day."

"I'm just grateful that we didn't end up like those poor souls, being mangled by an angry bear."

We glanced at the dead bodies around us. One man had been thrown a hundred yards, and had landed in a tree. His clothes were in shreds. The man in the black leather jacket had apparently died after being decapitated. The other three men, including the man in the red checkered scarf, were all lacking various parts of their anatomies. It was a gruesome sight.

We walked toward the hillside together.

"I wonder why the bear never attacked us?" I asked as we continued to follow in its footsteps. Then suddenly, the tracks just stopped.

"That's odd! The footprints just vanished."

Something clicked in my mind. "You don't suppose the bear is supernatural, do you?" I bit my lip. "In Navajo mythology, the bear is the most powerful of beasts. He always protects you."

"That could explain why they never used their weapons. They never had a chance."

The dogs kept sniffing the ground as they continued to search for the bear. Callista looked up at me, puzzled, her ice-blue eyes reflecting the light from the snow.

"I don't know what happened to that big hairy visitor. Maybe he went back to that timeless place. Maybe there is a gateway to heaven..." I was mesmerized as I looked at the big sky.

"Señora!" Pablo tugged at my shirt.

"What is it, Pablo? Just so you know, less than a year ago I was addressed as señorita," I said teasingly. "Seriously, I know you want to take us to the gravesite. Are you sure you want to reopen the wounds?"

The mere thought of what I was about to see gave me shivers.

"Oh, please, señorita!"

"You do learn quickly," I said, unable to resist a grin. "Okay, I'm ready to go, although I have to admit I'm afraid of the outcome. I just pray that our belief in a higher power will help us to endure what lies ahead."

A few hundred yards away there was a small barn.

"This way!" Pablo motioned.

Disoriented by wandering through the dark cavern and tunnels, we moved to the side of an eroded hill that blocked our view of the surrounding terrain. I looked down, but I couldn't believe my eyes. In the ditch were the semi-charred remains of at least one hundred people.

It was terrible to see. The stench didn't help. I could only imagine the tremendous psychological impact it had had on Pablo. One man had apparently died with a bullet wound in his head. His boots were lying next to his skeletal remains. Amid the rubble we could see shoes, clothing, and even some jewelry. I turned my face away.

"I can't bear to look at this!"

Clint came over and held me. "Most of the casualties are victims of drug violence, although, according to what Pablo told us, there are also a lot of innocent, hard-working Mexican citizens in this heap."

"Come on, son." He put his hand on Pablo's head. "We've seen enough now."

"It's awful, isn't it?" Pablo's face was solemn. "I just wanted someone else to know."

Clint took me by the arm. "Let's go back to the cave. You'd better jot down your memories before you forget."

"I could never forget this."

Chapter V

As darkness engulfed the hillside, we walked back toward the cave, which was obscured by a low rock wall.

"I don't know about you, but *I* could use a drink," I said, sitting down on one of the rocks.

"If we get to my hideout early enough tonight, I will make you another tequila." Pablo's voice crackled with excitement.

"You mean we didn't finish that bottle last night?"

"We did! But I can make my own tequila—another thing my papa taught me. All I have to do is gather enough agave leaves, steam them, and shred them. Then we will have more tequila."

"I appreciate your hospitality, Pablo, but you're not going to have any more tequila." I tried to sound stern.

Clint sat down beside me. "It makes no sense to try to find our way back through the cave tonight, especially now that there's no imminent danger."

"You're right. Everyone's dead."

"I'll go get some firewood. You guys stay here and relax."

Pablo joined me where I was sitting at the mouth of the cave. "Tell me about your book," he said, his dark eyes wide with curiosity.

"Don't you ever get tired?" I asked.

"No."

"Okay. Have you ever read a murder mystery?"

"Not really."

"Usually in a murder mystery, the crime will be solved and the killer or killers are exposed and punished. But in my story, that didn't happen. Justice was never served. Whoever killed my brother has gotten away with it. Also, unlike most novels, my book was written as a fictionalized account of true events. It was inspired by a true story."

Maybe I should start writing fiction, I thought. *In fiction, nobody sins with impunity.*

"Do you think drugs were involved?" he asked.

"There's a good possibility," I said. "That's why we're so interested in finding out more about this Juárez Cartel. There could be a definite link."

Clint returned a few minutes later with an armful of firewood.

"Are you all right?" he asked.

"Yes, but my mind is still full of dead bodies."

"I know. It wasn't a pleasant experience."

Once we were deep enough into the cave, Clint built us a warm, cozy fire. After he was through, he rolled a rock over to where we were sitting. "Can I get in on this discussion?" he asked.

"Sure. During your tenure with the Texas Rangers, you must have had encounters with drug dealers. Let me ask you…Who in the Juárez Cartel could have been responsible for all this carnage?"

"Exactly who heads the Juárez Cartel is not entirely clear. Not even the DEA knows for sure, but we may be way off target."

Pablo looked at Clint with questioning eyes, so I clarified. "That's the Drug Enforcement Administration."

"I'm just not sure the Juárez Cartel is responsible. I'll tell you all I know," Clint promised as he started to describe the bloody regime of the drug cartels.

"Colombian traffickers routinely use Mexican drug organizations to help move drugs north across the U.S. border. In return, the Mexican cartels earn valuable cuts of the cocaine trade. This alliance allows the Mexican syndicates to double their power and their exportation business.

"As the Mexican cartels send greater quantities of drugs into the United States and the flow of drugs increases, there are naturally more murders. Most of the mayhem has been blamed on the lucrative Juárez Cartel, which is among Mexico's four largest cartels. Amando Carrillo Fuentes took over in 1992 from Rafael Aguilar Guajardo, who once was a former drug agent and was shot down in Cancún. After Carillo's death in 1997, gangsters in Juárez waged a fierce power struggle, murdering an estimated sixty people."

"There have always been scores of drug-related murders along the southwestern U.S. border. Many of the victims are not only traffickers, but supposed government informers. It's getting increasingly difficult for U.S. law officers to operate in Mexico because of fear and corruption. Just last week, my office informed me that men wearing state police uniforms held two undercover agents from the DEA and FBI at gunpoint. It's not something you should try to follow up on by yourself."

"I totally agree," I said. "That's why I have you to protect me."

"You're not thinking what I *think* you're thinking, are you?"

"Yes."

"That's absurd! We are *not* going to Juárez, and that's the end of it!" He rolled over onto his side and closed his eyes. "I'm going to get some sleep."

"Have it your way."

The next morning, I felt a hand on my shoulder. It was Clint.

"I'm sorry," he said. "I should've known better. The word *no* is not in your vocabulary."

"So, what do you want?"

"It's time to get up!" he said as he wiggled closer to me on his belly. "Can I have a little kiss?"

"No!" I growled. I couldn't bring myself to laugh, even though I wanted to.

"I guess I'll have to resort to my old tactics. Get her up!" he yelled to Wrangler and Callista, who came bounding in my direction.

"Oh, no!" I wailed as the dogs landed on top of me.

Clint gathered me up in his arms and planted a smacking kiss on my cheek.

"You win!" I cried. "But if you want my opinion, you beasts *all* deserve to go to the pound!"

Later I reached down and tied my shoelaces. "Are you ready?" I asked.

"Yes. The things I have to put up with," he grumbled.

"*You*? What about me?"

He put his arm around my waist and grinned.

"It's cold," I said, pressing my face into the warmth of his jacket. "It's the kind of cold that goes right through you. You know, Clint, if we ever get out of this place, I'd like to go on a picnic."

"You're making me hungry," he said as he bent down and kissed me. "I wish we had this cave all to ourselves."

"Señorita?" Pablo came up behind us.

"Just call me Sarah," I said as Clint and I continued to embrace.

"Señorita Sarah?" Pablo insisted.

"What is it, Pablo?"

When I turned around, he was holding a small black ledger book.

"Where did you find that?"

"In the corner of the cave, near my hideout."

"Let me see it."

He handed it to me.

"Do you need some light?" Clint stood over me with his flashlight. "I bet this is a drug ledger."

I opened it. The ledger was handwritten and initialed with the letters *TC*. It indicated that *TC* (also known as Taco) had transported hundreds of pounds of pot beginning in July 1995. The book also noted that marijuana was frequently exchanged for cocaine.

"I wonder how long this book has been in this cave?" I flipped through the pages. "The time frame is close to that of my brother's murder."

"There were always suspicions that drugs were involved," Clint said as he turned to Pablo, "but we never had any evidence—until now. Thanks to you, we're getting closer."

"The nature of the drug problem has changed," Clint said, explaining that illicit drug trafficking has shifted from crack cocaine to other drugs, including heroin and methamphetamine. "It's not the same problem that existed ten or even five years ago."

I handed the book to Clint. "Guard this with your life," I said. "Let's go!"

Callista almost knocked Wrangler over as she pushed him out of the way. "She gets along with other dogs as long as she gets to lead the pack," Clint explained.

A few minutes later, Callista discovered the entrails from a badly decomposed animal and began to roll in it. "Ew! Why do dogs *do* that?"

"According to my Uncle George, it evolved from their wild ancestors as a way of masking their natural predatory odor when stalking downwind prey."

Ten minutes later she came over and licked my face. "Did you have to do that?" I hated the thought of where her tongue had just been. "You're just filthy," I scolded her.

Clint smiled at me. "They are dogs, you know."

Then he put his arm around me. "I'm truly proud of you," he said. Turning toward Pablo, he smiled and gave him a hug. "You are quite the little trooper, too."

"Thank you, señor," Pablo said, emotion in his eyes.

It was good to be back at Pablo's quarters. It felt safer now, especially after the ordeal we'd just been through.

"I'm exhausted," I said right before I fell asleep.

Suddenly a voice called out of the dark. *"Intuition guides you, and you need to listen."* It was the voice of my deceased brother.

"Clayton!" I said unconsciously.

The image of my brother clung to my mind all night, weaving in and out of my dreams.

"Wake up, Sarah! You're dreaming."

"Okay, okay." I groped for my notebook to see if I had any proof that this whole thing wasn't a dream. I found a notation: *Listen to your sixth sense and you'll find the answers you're looking for.*

"Hmmm. I don't remember writing that." I sat there, completely puzzled and confused. "Still, the fact is, strange and inexplicable things happen in our lives every day. We usually tend to reject them because they are out of our reality."

"No kidding!"

Still groggy with sleep, I yawned. "Is it morning already?"

"Almost, sleepyhead."

"I hope we're not going to have to crawl through that miserable tunnel again in order to get out of here."

"Maybe we can find the way Callista came in."

"I'll be ready in a few minutes."

"Don't push yourself."

"Are you going to call the police when we get out of here?"

"I'm going to call the FBI about the gravesite, but as to those other sleazy bastards, as far as I'm concerned, they can rot."

"What's going to become of me now that this is over?" Pablo's eyes reflected his fear.

"Don't worry, son. We're not going to leave you alone."

The dogs led the way into a low tunnel branching off the artery that we had followed after our escape from the safe room. A dim light appeared ahead of us. When we reached the opening, Clint raised his head and gave me the all clear.

"I'm right behind you," I yelled, brushing the dirt from my clothes. "I can't wait to get out of here."

Outside, the sky began to lighten. The birds filled the air with their songs, heralding the dawn. A shrine of winter flowers blossomed through the patches of snow-packed ground.

For a moment we just looked at one another. I was so glad that we were all alive! As we emerged from the tunnel and made our way toward the trading post, I could see the burial grounds where Pablo's family lay. I said a silent prayer. Then I realized exactly where we were located. I stopped, looking around in a circle.

"Clint, this is ridiculous!" I yelled. "We didn't have to go through that stupid tunnel at all. Look where we are!"

"So much for my Indian direction instinct," he said. "Come on, Sarah. You can give me a hard time later."

We circled back to the front of the trading post. I couldn't believe my eyes. Our vehicle was parked in the exact same spot where we had left it.

"Get in!" Clint shouted as he called for the dogs. "Load 'em up! We should be at the motel in about an hour."

"Just think: soon I can have a nice warm bath!"

There was snow on the side of the road, little patches here and there. "Maybe I'm wrong, but I think that's a snow cloud," I said, glancing up at the sky.

"We'd better keep an eye on the weather. If we get too much snow over the weekend, we might not be able to get home."

We drove to the only motel we could see with a Vacancy sign.

"Do you suppose they allows pets?"

"I haven't the vaguest idea. I'm sure they're going to think we're a bunch of vagabonds. We'd better not press our luck."

Clint paid for two adjoining rooms. Thank goodness he still had his wallet. Then he handed me his credit card. "Get anything you want, beautiful."

"As soon as we get settled, I'm going straight down to the gift shop to buy some clothes."

"That's a good idea. I'm sure we could all use some new clothes."

We decided to sneak the dogs up the back staircase to our room. Then we went down to the lobby. "The gift shop is over this way," Pablo said excitedly.

The desk clerk shot a hostile look at Pablo.

"He's with us," I said.

I selected some lingerie, a ribbed turtleneck, a sweater, two pairs of jeans, and a leather car coat. Before I was through, I threw in some suede ankle boots, a great wardrobe staple.

Pablo and Clint were in the men's section. They each selected a warm fleece-lined jacket, jeans, and some trendy sweatshirts. "Don't forget the socks and underwear," I said as the clerk rang up my purchases and put them in a bag.

We headed back to our rooms. "As soon as I get these clothes off, I'm going to throw them in the trash. I suggest you do the same."

Clint went over and opened the door to the adjoining bedroom.

"Is this my room?" Pablo asked as he peeked in.

"Yes," Clint nodded.

"*Mio Dios!*" Pablo said, impressed.

"If there's anything you need, we'll be right here. Now go get cleaned up so that we can have dinner."

"What will we have?" Pablo asked.

"I don't know. What would you like?"

"Pizza!"

"Pizza!" I screamed from the bathroom. "We've been starving for nearly five days, and you want *pizza*?"

Later that evening, we walked over to the restaurant. After we were seated, I turned to the waitress with a plaintive look. "Do you serve pizza?"

"No," she smiled. "But there are a lot of other good things on the menu. Tonight's special is barbecued ribs."

"How does that sound, Pablo?"

"Not as good as pizza," he complained.

We all ordered the ribs. After we finished, we ordered another plate for the dogs and a doggie bag to go. "We don't always bring back bones for the dogs," I explained. "Nor do we always appease a whining child by giving him what he wants. We all know the consequences of exceedingly tolerant behavior."

Pablo shrugged.

"I can see that made a big impression!" Clint laughed.

"I'll tell you what," I continued. "If there's pizza being served anywhere in this town, we'll find it tomorrow."

"Yeah!" Pablo grinned.

I felt like a parent again.

The next morning, when we woke up, Clint reached for the phone. "I'm going to call the office to see if the Texas Rangers want to get involved in this case. If not, I'm sure they'll refer me to the proper authorities."

"It's shocking to think about what that poor kid has gone through," he said as he waited on the line.

He spoke with his former boss.

"They prefer not to get involved. However, they agreed to monitor the investigation. My boss said he would personally update us each day. He also said he would contact the U.S. Border Patrol and the other various agencies."

Later that morning, as the three of us walked out of the room, a throng of reporters converged on us, wanting to hear about the boy who'd lived in a cave.

"I'd say your boss did a pretty good job of notifying everyone," I whispered to Clint.

Every agency imaginable was there. There were representatives from the DEA, FBI, Bureau of Indian Affairs, and the Border Patrol. The television crews were just arriving.

"Can you tell us about it, son?" A reporter shoved a microphone in Pablo's face. "Start from the beginning."

"My family wanted to come to the U.S. and find work, but my parents could not get visas. They asked the Coyotes to help us."

"Do you remember what the Coyotes looked like? Do you think you could identify them?"

"No," Pablo said, choking back tears. "But I can still hear the cruel words of the guards as they tortured and killed those people."

I looked around. There wasn't a dry eye in the crowd after he was through telling his story.

The Border Patrol Agent looked over at Clint. "Can you take me to the gravesite?"

"Certainly. You can ride with us if you'd like."

"I'd appreciate it."

"This is my wife, Sarah. I'm Clint Walkerman."

"Nice to meet you." I shook his hand.

"Please call me Chief. Everybody else does."

We walked over to the truck. Pablo and I were relegated to the back seat of the extended cab.

"I assume you drove up here this morning?" Clint began.

"Yes. After hearing the news, I canceled all my appointments for the day. Luckily, I was already part of the way here, in Grants, New Mexico."

He told Clint that efforts to smuggle illegal aliens into the U.S. had escalated. "The problem is a considerable one for us," he admitted, citing illegal immigration, drug trafficking, and new fears of terrorism. "The reality is that we desperately need more agents. And stiffer penalties," he added.

When we arrived at the trading post, another truck was already parked in the lot.

"I guess the Feds beat us to it!" Chief smiled as he got out of the truck.

We went over to the trading post and stood in the eerie emptiness. "This is quite a spectacular place. It reminds me of something out of the past. Too bad the walls can't talk."

"If only you knew."

We followed the contour of the mountain and walked over to where the hillside dropped away. The Feds had used a helicopter to scour the gravesite by air; it was obviously closer to the post than we had thought. Narcotics officers from the DEA wearing masks and gloves were already standing amid the corpses, sifting through them.

"Wow, this is tough to look at," Chief said, turning around. I think I'm going to be sick."

"We should probably leave you inspectors to your work," Clint said.

Just as we were about to leave, two investigators from the Bureau of Indian Affairs pulled into the driveway.

"What a fiasco this is going to be!" Clint predicted.

We drove back to the motel. There was a note stuck to our door from the Immigration and Naturalization Service. They wanted to talk to Pablo.

"I guess we'll deal with that tomorrow," Clint sighed.

"You never got your pizza," I reminded Pablo. "Maybe we can find some tonight."

"I don't feel like eating."

"Why?" I asked, genuinely stumped.

Pablo opened the door to his adjoining bedroom. "Would it be all right if the dogs slept with me tonight?"

"Sure. As long as you don't let them get in bed with you. That will upset the maids. I think they already know we have dogs. Would you like us to bring you something back from the restaurant?"

"No, thank you. I'm just going to go to bed."

I watched Pablo close his door with a soft thud. "Poor kid. He desperately misses his family."

Clint and I went out to dinner by ourselves and had a lovely time.

"Maybe we can go home tomorrow," I said as we drove back to the motel.

"We'll see what tomorrow brings."

First thing the next morning, I knocked on Pablo's door. There was no answer. I tried the doorknob, but it was locked. *Where could he be?* I didn't even hear the dogs, and I knew that they had slept with him last night.

"Don't worry," Clint said. "He's got to be around here somewhere. Let's go down to the restaurant. Maybe he's already there."

When we arrived, there was no sign of Pablo.

"Let's order something that can be prepared quickly," I said as I looked at the menu. "I'm really getting concerned about him."

I decided on the scrambled eggs. They arrived on my plate fried and sunny-side up.

"I used to get upset when people made small mistakes; now they don't even faze me."

When we went back up to the room, I knocked on Pablo's door again. Still no answer. Then I heard a thump of a tail.

"That's Wrangler! Do you have a key to Pablo's room?" I asked Clint.

"No. I gave him the only key we had."

"We'd better go down to the office then. I'm sure the manager has an extra key."

No such luck, but the manager was gracious enough to let us in with his master key. When he opened the door, I thought I'd die of embarrassment.

There was Callista with her head on the pillow, and Wrangler relaxing at the foot of the bed.

The manager cleared this throat. "You *do* know that dogs are not allowed in this motel?"

"I'm sorry," I said. "I didn't know. We'll be glad to pay any extra charges."

"There won't be any extra charges, but I'm going to have to ask you to get rid of those dogs."

I looked around the room and began to cry. "What are we going to do?"

"Okay, okay," the manager relented, giving me a stiff nod. "They can stay for *one* more night. But that's *it*," he grumbled as he closed the door.

"At least we got over that hurdle! Where's Pablo?" I asked Wrangler and Callista as I softly petted them.

"We have to face it," Clint answered. "Pablo is gone."

He went off to file a missing person's report with the Apache County Sheriff's Office while I sat down on the staircase outside and sobbed. "Why would Pablo leave?"

When Clint returned, he came over and comforted me. For the next few hours, we sat in silence and waited. A light rain that would probably turn into snow later that night forced us to abandon our perch and go inside.

Clint went over to the phone to see if there were any messages.

"Any word yet?"

"No."

"Pablo is probably going to starve to death. It's almost dinnertime and he hasn't eaten since yesterday."

"Speaking of dinner, let's just order room service."

"That's fine with me," I said as I looked out the window at the black sky.

Clint picked up the phone and placed our order. As we waited, I voiced the scenario that was emerging in my mind.

"Just suppose there was a little boy out there braving the nighttime chill, wandering around like a stray dog in a town of strangers. There's no one to tuck him into bed. He was probably afraid that because he didn't have the proper papers, he would be returned to his native country."

"Don't underestimate Pablo. He has more street sense than you do. I think your scenario is correct, though. I'm sure he is concerned about his legal status and worried that he might be taken into custody or deported."

After we finished dinner, Clint put on his jacket.

"Where are you going?" I asked.

"I'm going to see if I can find a newspaper. I'd like to catch up on what's been going on."

Later that night, as we crawled into bed, Callista was lying with her head on the pillow. "Move over," I said as I rubbed her belly.

"You're spoiling her," Clint grumbled as he opened the paper.

"You're just jealous," I teased.

"Oh, no!" Clint exclaimed. "It looks like all hell broke loose in the Four Corners area, complete with a car chase and a shoot-out. I think John Morgan, may have been shot, too."

"You can't be serious!"

"According to one witness, a truck pulled up beside a police car. A man in a camouflage jacket jumped out and fired six shots through the windshield. One of the bullets grazed Deputy John Morgan's head. Another sheriff's deputy, who was also in the car, was unharmed."

"It's too bad that gunman didn't blow Morgan's head off!"

"Now, now, is that any way for a nice girl to talk?"

"If Morgan wants to play rough, so can other people."

Clint folded the newspaper and turned off the lights. "Let's go to bed and see how nice you *really* are."

I lay stretched out on the bed, listening to the night sounds coming in through the window. Clint leaned across me, his face very close to mine. I could feel his manly endowment pressing against me as he gently ran his hands down my body. As always, it immediately responded to his loving embrace.

Afterward, still breathless, I kissed him softly. "It was only once," I whispered teasingly. "And it was tremendous. But you know me. Only once is like Chinese food. An hour later, and I'm hungry again!"

He laughed. Later on, I massaged his shoulder and confessed I couldn't sleep.

"For God's sake, Sarah! We can't do this all night. I'm not as young as I used to be!"

"But you don't want me to worry about Pablo all by myself, do you?"

He didn't.

After a fitful night, I wondered if I would ever sleep soundly again. My life had changed so drastically that I scarcely recognized myself when I looked in the mirror. Now that we had missed Thanksgiving, I began thinking about Christmas. Was it only eight years ago that I had been anticipating spending Christmas with my family in Phoenix?

In other happier years, we had enjoyed celebrating the holiday at the cabin, with piles of wrapped gifts for one another stacked around the crèche on the hearth. We invited guests for dinner, and also houseguests for the week. There was always a feast for my sons' friends who lived in Phoenix, as well as their parents, who frequently came up to the mountains to be with us.

But Christmas had not been the same since we had lost Clayton. I had tried very hard for Preston's and Conner's sakes to keep up our traditions: decorating the house with bright wreaths of juniper, making my own mimosa cocktails, and shelling shrimp for brunch.

This year I anticipated a happier holiday with Clint beside me at the house in Cornflower Corners. My Christmas presents for Preston and Conner, their wives, and my grandchildren were still in bags packed in the truck. I also had a belated birthday gift I had purchased at the gift shop for my granddaughter. *Would they ever receive their presents?*

This time of year, people everywhere were preparing for the holiday season. I wished we could just go home. I could feel myself becoming melancholic. At this sentimental time of year, my mind traveled back to a long-ago Christmas. It was the very last time we saw my brother.

Clayton was putting more wood on the fire, holding his hands to the warmth as the rest of us gathered around the tree.

He was so fond of his nephews, and we talked about what they were doing in college.

"Whatever you do, Sarah, don't let your sons grow up to be lawyers," Clayton grinned. We started to laugh. "There are enough unemployed attorneys in the family!"

It was moments like this—the conversation, the family stories—that were the true legacy of all those dinners we shared every holiday season. We were such a normal, happy family back then. How could it have been shattered so completely?

Most people I knew had lost loved ones. Was my continued obsession with it because I didn't know why it had happened or who had done it? Did the empty feeling linger because justice had not been served?

Anxious about Pablo, Clint and I decided to take breakfast in our room in case he returned. On impulse, I picked up the phone and called Conner in Colorado. "I just wanted to hear about your day, and to tell you that I love you and miss you."

Then I did the same thing with Preston in Phoenix.

"Mom! Where have you been?" His voice was frantic. "We've been so worried! We knew you wouldn't miss your granddaughter's birthday unless something terrible had happened."

"You wouldn't believe it, even if I told you. Don't worry, though, I'm okay."

I contacted Mother next, dreading the call. I knew she was going to be upset, especially because I had left her with the hectic job of managing the RV Park. I was right.

After I placed my calls, I went back to the window. Clint walked over to where I was standing. "Please hold me."

"Gladly."

Later that morning, we met with the FBI.

"Do you think Pablo was abducted?" the agent asked.

"I doubt it. I think he ran away."

Finally, toward the end of the day, we received some good news. One of the maids had seen Pablo standing near the motel dumpster earlier that day. She had recognized him from his TV celebrity status.

"That means he's still around here," I said. "I'm going to take the dogs for a walk. I have a strong feeling that Pablo is alive. He's probably struggling, scared, and maybe hurt, but I believe he's trying to get help and find his way back here."

"Do you want me to go with you?"

"No. You'd better stay here and wait for any further news."

After we left the motel, the dogs and I walked along the main roadway. "Go find Pablo!" I commanded them. Wrangler and Callista began sniffing the ground. When we came to a red light, they stopped. Suddenly they made a mad dash for an open field. "This is not the time to hunt for gophers!" I shouted after them.

A short distance away, there was an irrigation ditch. I followed the dogs as they ran in that direction. "Wait for me!" I yelled. By the time I caught up with them, all I could see were their two tails wagging. Both of their heads were embedded in a huge irrigation pipe.

I heard a tiny voice. It was Pablo.

"Sarah, I really need your help. I think I may have twisted my ankle," he said as he stuck his head out of the opening.

When he finally emerged from the pipe, the dogs were all over him. "Back up and give him some room!"

"Pablo," I said with tears in my eyes. "Don't you ever do this again!"

I was desperate to pass on the news to Clint.

"You wait here," I instructed Pablo. "I'll be right back. I'll leave the dogs with you."

I practically flew back to the motel.

"Guess what?" I said as Clint opened the door. "I have some incredible news!"

"You've found him."

"Yes!"

"Where is he?"

"He's sitting in a field next to an irrigation ditch"

"Is he all right?"

"Yes, but I think he injured his ankle."

"Let's go," Clint said, and grabbed his keys.

We jumped into the truck.

"Where's this field?" he asked.

"It's a mile or so down the road."

Within a few minutes, we came to the light.

"They're over there," I pointed.

"I think I can see them."

Clint pulled the truck up to the ditch.

"Hello, Señor Clint," Pablo said sheepishly.

"Hello, son."

"I'm so sorry!" Pablo cried. "I'll never run away again!" He sobbed as Clint carried him back to the truck.

After a quick trip to the emergency room, we went back to the motel.

"You get some rest now," I said as I fluffed his pillows. "And remember what the doctor said. Stay off that foot."

"Yeah, I know." He gave me a tentative smile.

Later that evening, I peeked inside his door. He was wide awake.

"Guess what?" I said as I walked in. "You don't need to be plagued by that relentless craving for pizza any longer."

I handed him a large box containing a pepperoni pizza. "The restaurant made this especially for you."

"Just for me?"

"Yes."

Clint and I rose early the next morning. "I'll let you in on a little secret," he said as he put his arms around me. "We're going home today."

"You mean it? We're really going home?" I said, perking up.

"Yes. And I'll let you in on another secret, too. From there, we're going to Juárez."

"Wait until my family hears this news!"

"What about Pablo? Is he going with us?"

"Yes, but…"

"But what?"

"When we get to Juárez, he's probably going to have to remain there. I spoke with his aunt this morning. She wants him to come home. She told me she would treat him like a member of her family."

"I hate to think of how Pablo is going to take this news."

"We're about to find out," Clint said as he walked into the room.

"Please sit down, son," Clint began. "We're going to take you back to Cornflower Corners with us for a few days. From there, we're going to Juárez."

Pablo sat straight in the chair, his arms crossed tightly on his chest.

"I spoke with your Aunt Seledonia today. She would like you to come back home and live with her and her family."

"She would?" Pablo's eyes grew bright. "My Aunt Seledonia lives on a farm. She has all kinds of animals. That will be fun!"

"That was easy." I smiled over at Clint.

"Now, go get your things together, Pablo, and we'll be on our way."

"*Sí*, señorita!" he yelled.

After putting on my new suede ankle boots and flinging my new leather car coat over my shoulders, I walked out the door.

"We'd better get some gas," Clint said as he pulled the truck into a station.

While he went about it, the attendant spoke to me. "You'd better be careful driving around here. There's a lot of black ice on the road. Ice is a funny thing," he said.

"What do you mean?"

"It's just very unpredictable. It's not unusual for people to fall through weak ice. It happens all the time. Ice thickness, when it comes to strength, means nothing. It's actually the *quality* of the ice. Snow just complicates the picture: it can protect strong, thick ice, but it can also insulate the surface against freezing and cover up weak ice.

"Just this morning, some guy drove his snowmobile across an open lake and fell through some thin ice. Last I heard, the paramedics were still trying to revive him."

"How horrible," I said, getting back into the truck.

"What was that all about?" Clint asked.

"I'm not sure. From what I could gather, some guy tried to cut across a partially frozen lake and fell through some thin ice."

"When I was a child, my family never crossed a lake or a river without prayers and corn pollen, the traditional Navajos' offering to the Holy People. It would ensure a safe journey for my family. I used to carry it with me all the time."

"That's probably not a bad idea," I said, mostly to myself.

The snow began to fall. I took one last look at the stark, remote beauty and the forty-five-mile stretch of canyon walls. I gazed at the white, anvil-shaped clouds, the red rocks and the villages with names that sounded like an ancient millennium.

CHAPTER VI

"I can't believe we're really home," I said as we stood on the deck at the back doorway. I noticed Mother had it decorated for Christmas.

"Please come in, Pablo, and make yourself at home."

It didn't take long for him to settle in. The next time I looked, he was in front of the television set, feasting on a plate of chips and salsa.

"Do you mind if I turn the TV to the news station?" I asked. "I'd like to see what's been happening with the weather."

"Well, folks!" the newscaster began. "Winter has finally arrived in the high country. Once the snow starts flying, the emergency calls start coming in. Just this morning, some thrill-seeking snowmobile rider attempted to shoot across a frozen lake and fell through some thin ice into frigid water. It was the first death of the season attributed to a fall through ice since last year, when two fishermen fell into a pond. The fire department's rescue team would like to caution everyone that no ice is safe."

Then a picture of the man who plunged to his death into the freezing water flashed on screen.

Good grief! It was Jerome Kramer. I almost fainted.

"Clint!" I screamed.

"What is it?" he asked as he came flying into the room.

"Listen to this!" I turned the volume up on the TV.

The broadcast continued.

"The man who died today was Jerome Kramer, a local resident. At one time he used to own and operate the Blue Sage Trading Post. Our viewers may recall that Kramer's partner was murdered at that trading post nearly eight years ago."

Clint sat there dumbfounded. "Run that by me one more time. Was that *Jerome Kramer* they were talking about?"

"You heard it right. He's dead."

"That must have been the same guy the attendant was talking about."

"Do you think his death is a coincidence?" I asked.

"Given the circumstances, I'd say there is a good likelihood that this was the work of a diabolical spirit."

"I hope it isn't an omen of things to come."

We stayed in Cornflower Corners just long enough to take Pablo fly-fishing. For the longest time, I didn't understand what the big deal was about fly-fishing. I knew it was a recreational sport, but there were a lot of other sports that seemed more exciting.

It wasn't until I learned to cast a fly so that it would float over the still waters where the fish were swimming that I realized its appeal. On a particularly pleasant afternoon, situated in a sunny spot, it seemed as if I existed outside of time.

My troubles simply vanished. They faded into the shimmering, deep-purple crevices of the canyon walls that surrounded me. "With any luck, in a moment of distraction, I might even *catch* a fish!"

The next day we packed our bags. I put on my favorite tee shirt, one that my son Conner had brought back for me from one of his trips abroad. *This is going to be fun.*

"Once we get to El Paso, are we going to drive across the border?"

"I don't think so. We'll probably take a cab as I don't want to take our new jeep across."

I turned around and looked at Pablo, who was sitting in the back seat. "Just think. In less than five hours, you'll be home. And just in time for Christmas, too." I smiled.

As we drove, Pablo remained quiet.

When we arrived at the Mexican border, Clint parked the jeep in an open lot. We were immediately ushered into a drug-screening building. Pablo tearfully told U.S. Custom officials that he wanted to go home. We spent the better part of the day there. First they talked about putting Pablo in a foster home or a youth shelter in Juárez, just until they could determine who had legal custody of him. Finally, immigration officials just decided to release him to his family. I suspect it was because of all the notoriety he had received.

After we passed through the inspection station and crossed over the bridge to the Mexican side of the border, we hailed a taxi. Just as we were about to get in, we heard some shouting.

"Hurry up and get in!" the cab driver yelled. "It sounds like the Border Patrol may have found some drugs. Both sides of the border will be tied up for hours! You should've seen the logjam last night when they seized over twelve hundred pounds of marijuana from two vehicles abandoned by drivers who fled on foot into Mexico."

"That was dumb on their part," Pablo said. "Just like the carpet walkers."

"I beg your pardon!"

"Carpet walkers," he repeated. "You know, those smugglers who sneak across the border with drugs on their backs and carpet squares on their feet so they don't leave prints."

"You're right, kid," the cab driver murmured. "I used to have two friends who were carpet walkers. They thought they could get away with it, but they were found dead."

We drove along the narrow cobblestone streets and then came to a small shantytown where people were living in cardboard and tin houses.

The cab driver turned to me. "Smuggling across the border is nothing new. For years, banditos, Apaches, bootleggers, and gunrunners have all carved black-market routes along this western frontier. Some of the inroads, I'm told, date back to Geronimo's day.

"It's a shame," he said. "But I understand why poor campesinos take jobs as smugglers. They're accustomed to making four dollars a day, if they can find work. They're not blind; they see how their American counterparts live. So, they agree to carry one load of cocaine or pot across the line and hope they don't get caught. They come home with more money than they would earn in a year. That allows them to pay the rent."

We continued to drive south across a vast swath of prickly pear desert. When we finally came to an old pueblo, the driver stopped.

"Is this where your Aunt Seledonia lives?"

"*Sí*," Pablo said.

"You were right about one thing," I smiled. "She really does have a lot of animals."

There were geese, chickens, and guinea hens parading about. There were also rabbits, pigs, cows, goats, and sheep. It looked like a petting zoo!

Over in the corral stood a pair of fine horses. "I definitely think you are in good hands." I winked at Pablo.

His aunt was ecstatic to see him. "*Grácias, grácias, grácias*," she said to me as she hugged him.

"I guess we'll be on our way then," Clint said. "We have some business to attend to while we're here."

Pablo broke down in tears. "I don't want you to go!"

"Hang in there, sweetie! It gets better with time." I picked him up and hugged him tight.

"We'll see you again soon."

Clint and I took the same cab back to town. As we made it back across the border I turned toward him. "Where are we going next?"

"To the Attorney General's Office. Maybe he can enlighten us as to who the kingpins are in this smuggling operation. I'm sure there's a branch office in El Paso."

Luckily, the Attorney General was in and able to see us. After we exchanged pleasantries, Clint asked him for any information he could give us about drug smuggling into Northern Arizona.

"Arizona is fast becoming a major artery for drug traffic coming across the border," he began, "and no one expects it to stop. There's just too much money to be made. Pot, methamphetamines, and heroin all roll across the southern border so fast and in such large quantities that almost every part of the state is affected.

"There are three principle players," he informed us, "although I don't know their names. Dealers seldom use their real names, relying instead on nicknames. On a rural reservation where unemployment is high and job opportunities are scarce, a smuggler's cash is alluring. I can understand why the local residents would be tempted. They stand to make a great deal of money if they just stash the drugs until drivers can take them to urban warehouses.

"Most of the drugs that are destined for the Navajo Indian Reservation are shipped out of Texas and New Mexico. The high desert between New Mexico and Arizona is prime smuggling turf. It's well off the beaten track, yet offers smugglers access to roads leading directly to interstate freeways and cities like Phoenix, Tucson, and Los Angeles.

"Drug dealers in this area are becoming increasingly sophisticated in the ways they send hot shipments over the line. They pack drugs into just about anything, including dead bodies. It's hard to keep a handle on it. The trouble is," he grimaced, "the drivers usually know very little about where the drugs came from or where they're going.

"The system keeps Mexican sources and U.S. warehouses from being discovered if the drugs are busted en route. Acting on a tip from one of our informers, our inspectors were able to capture and detain a known drug trafficker named Taco. However, he was able to escape. We are conducting a full investigation and will follow up with appropriate action based on our findings," he said.

"You needn't bother. He's dead." Clint explained what had happened at the cave. We thanked the Attorney General for his time and information, and promised to let him know of any new developments that we might find.

When we left his office, I told Clint it was time for some dinner and a hotel. I didn't feel like traveling eight more hours confined inside a vehicle. Thankfully, he agreed.

We found a hotel, registered, and went next door to a cute country restaurant. Dinner was relaxing, and for once Clint didn't talk about drug smuggling. We made our way back to our room, and as I was undressing, he looked at me with an intense look in his eyes.

"I love you so much. Now why don't you show me just how much *you love me?*"

I smiled, dropped my clothes, and lay on the bed. Clint fell into my arms.

After driving on what seemed like an endless succession of freeways the next day, we arrived home.

"I don't know about you, but I'm ready to rest for a while."

"What you need is a little exercise." Clint started his vigorous workout regime. "Would you care to join me?"

"Are you out of your mind?" I snapped. "I get as much pleasure from exercise as I get from banging my head against a wall. In both cases, it feels best when I stop. I'll just turn the TV on. Maybe I can find some news. Besides, after last night, I don't think I really need any exercise!"

"We interrupt this broadcast to bring you the latest news on the shootings in the Four Corners area," the newscaster said, clutching the wire service reports in his hand.

"Armed with a shotgun and a stolen Ford pickup, the man was unstoppable. He rammed his way through two police cars and rear-ended two parked vehicles. Instead of fleeing, it almost seemed as if he were determined to kill Deputy John Morgan…"

"Clint!" I yelled. "I think Morgan was involved in another shoot-out."

"No way!" I heard him shout from the other room.

"Hurry up before you miss this!" I shouted as the newscaster continued to deliver the news.

"The fatal chase apparently began when Officer John Morgan from the Apache County Sheriff's Department began his wild pursuit of a stolen Ford truck. Even when a cadre of police cornered the disabled vehicle in the parking lot of the Tomahawk Trading Post, the man refused to surrender. Instead, he reached for a rifle on the passenger seat and took deadly aim at John Morgan. That's when DPS Officer John Smith opened fire, but it was too late.

"Witnesses reported hearing up to six rifle shots. Deputy John Morgan was faced with a similar situation last week when a bullet grazed his head. This time, he was unable to dodge the bullet. One bullet ripped through his arm, another went straight into his chest. Luckily he was wearing a Kevlar vest. Otherwise, he would be dead."

"Step up to the plate. This is ball two," Clint grinned. "The bases are loaded and there's still nobody out."

"What are you talking about?"

"If Morgan wants to play hardball, so can I."

"This is insane. You didn't have anything to do with this! Did you?"

"Not directly."

"I didn't realize that by returning a curse, we were creating a monster."

"Get used to it."

Hours later, I awoke to the telephone ringing. The clock next to my bed read 3:20 a.m. Clint groggily grabbed the receiver as I sat up, suddenly alert. I crawled over to his side of the bed.

"Quiet," Clint whispered as he pressed his index finger over his lips. He turned on the speakerphone. It was his former boss.

"I just got off the phone with John Morgan. He called me from his hospital bed. He sounds like he's in pretty bad shape, both mentally and physically. I don't know how this guy knows you, or why he thinks you've done something to him. I've just spent the last two hours listening to him babble about a curse. He kept ranting that it was some sort of a vendetta."

Clint began to laugh. "They're probably giving him too many drugs at the hospital."

"So you don't know anything about it?"

"No," Clint paused, "not really."

"I didn't think so. I'm sorry to have bothered you."

"That wasn't exactly the truth." I looked over at Clint.

"As far as I'm concerned, it was. If I told him the truth about the curse of the *Chindi*, he'd have me committed to a looney bin!"

***

The next day, Clint spoke to his boss again.

"You won't believe this," he said as we listened to him on the speakerphone again. "Morgan apparently injured himself last night during a violent nightmare. He dreamed he was in a deep hole filled with giant spiders. Terror-stricken, he jumped out of bed and ran into a wall, bruising his already injured arm. They're going to transfer him to a rehab facility in about two weeks. He's already begun working with therapists."

"Big spiders, you say?"

"Abnormal fears are no laughing matter," his boss retorted. "Many of us are deathly afraid of crawly things."

"You're right, sir. I know this sounds crazy, but Sarah's brother was found in a deep hole filled with spiders after he was murdered."

"That really gives me the chills," his boss said. "One more thing, and then I'll let you go. The gunman who shot Morgan apparently has been busted before. Although we're waiting on fingerprints to confirm his identity, we're ninety-nine percent sure it's a guy who goes by the nickname Juggler."

I leaned forward, interested. The police had considered someone named Juggler a prime suspect in my brother's murder, too.

Clint's boss continued. "A dragon on our assailant's chest and a *J* on his wrist match descriptions we have of Juggler's tattoos. His rap sheet shows previous arrests for both robbery and car theft."

That news gave *me* the chills.

Later that same afternoon, my son Preston called from Phoenix.

"Mom! Have you been listening to the news?"

"Yes, I know. Morgan was shot."

"Is that the same Morgan who was in charge of Clayton's homicide investigation?"

"Yes, the very same."

"Wow! I never made the connection. Apparently there's more strange stuff going on at the reservation. The TV stations are broadcasting live coverage from the scene of an accident that occurred last night at Clayton's old trading post. You'd better turn on the news."

"I'll do that right now. Thanks, Preston."

"An official from the Navajo Nation reports that last night, in the middle of the most desolate place you've ever laid your eyes upon, two members of the same clan rolled their vehicle off the side of the mountain. Both were residents of the area and had previously worked at the Blue Sage Trading Post."

As the reporter spoke, the camera panned past the trading post. Ice still glittered on the road. "The freak accident occurred at two o'clock in the morning. One man died instantly in the fiery explosion. The other, suffering massive head injuries and burns, was rushed to the hospital. I interviewed him as he lay dying. He gave his name as Lenny and indicated that his death came to him in a dream, like a supernatural vision. He motioned me closer and whispered that he wanted to confess something."

This should be good, I thought.

"He admitted to starting a blaze in a restaurant. His dying words were: 'It was my own dark deeds that led me to this.' He also revealed the acts that he believed had led him to his ultimate fate. He spoke a Navajo prayer used to combat emotional trauma and fend off evil. Then he died.

"So there you have it, folks" the newscaster said, wrapping up his report. "If you didn't think life was mysterious before, you might now. If you think that everything in life is a coincidence, it may be time to reconsider."

"What do you make of all this?" I looked at Clint. "I still believe that Kramer was the responsible party behind the scenes, and the person who probably put them up to it."

"They will call this poetic justice. The way I see it is that we all make choices in our lives. The hardest lesson to learn is which bridge to burn and which bridge to cross. They obviously chose the wrong one."

"You're right, but at least they confirmed they started the fire."

"Don't trust them. They would like you to believe that they had no involvement in your brother's murder, but we both know that's a lie. Don't be deceived by them."

"I know what you mean. My book has taken a frightening turn. The murderers in my story, most notably John Morgan, are rightfully paranoid and unconscionably free of guilt. They're only afraid of getting caught. The deed doesn't haunt them, and no amount of coercion will ever force a confession."

"Don't worry," Clint said with his usual quiet confidence. "Sooner or later, someone will spill the beans. If they live long enough."

"Just the same," I said, "this blood lust has got to stop. I think everyone named as a suspect in my book is involved. So what's going to happen to them? Are they all going to die?"

"Confession is good for the soul, but my demon seeks an unquenchable amount of vengeance." Clint had a strange look in his eyes. "Four little, three little, two little Indians," he began to sing. "And then there was none."

"Quit that!" I said angrily. "I'm not in the mood for teasing."

"I'm sorry," he said. "Come here and let me rub your shoulders."

"Oh," I sighed. "That feels good."

"You're the most fascinating woman I've ever met." He kissed the back of my neck.

"Flattery will get you everywhere."

"It will?"

That night was one of the most enchanting evenings we'd ever spent together. "Honey," I murmured amorously as I kissed him. "I'm so glad I have you as my lifelong companion."

"Now *I'm* the one who's feeling flattered," he said as he kissed me back.

We ended up going out to the quirky local restaurant which had amazing things on the menu. We ignored the hamburgers and tacos. Clint ordered rattlesnake and I had frog legs. As the waiter brought us our dinner, I looked down at my plate. "Do you suppose animals have consciousness?"

"What made you think of that?"

"Never mind." I carefully cut into a piece of frog leg with my fork and then gingerly put it into my mouth and swallowed it.

Clint snorted with laughter. "Just be glad you didn't order the rainbow trout. You'd have to look it in the eye!"

"Laugh all you want to," I said coolly. "But I'm sure glad we evolved to have consciousness! It allows us to combine the input from different senses, letting us construct objects in our mind.

"A frog, for example, has a mechanical reflex to snap at any dark moving object of a certain size. That same frog would starve to death, even in the midst of a heap of freshly killed flies, because it doesn't recognize them as flies by vision or any other sense.

"Consciousness may have been adapted to allow our ancestors to picture what other members of their social group were thinking about and planning to do next, a very handy function when it comes to survival. Without consciousness, we would all find ourselves like sleepwalkers; able to function, yet unaware of our presence in the world. This makes me wonder…are dogs really awake when they chase rabbits? Or are they like sleepwalkers who drive off in their cars in the middle of the night?"

"You're crazy as hell." Clint reached over and held my hand. "Maybe that's why I love you. By the way, when did you become an expert on amphibians?" he chuckled.

"While I was thinking about the human mind and the rest of the natural world, I realized that I believe in evolution, which doesn't conflict with the creation story in my mind.

"But that's not to say that the universe wasn't created by an intelligent design. It just took God a little longer than seven days and seven nights to accomplish his goal, or perhaps God's days were a little longer than they are now. That's all. For Him to try to explain that it took billions of years to create the world to the first people, who still believed the earth was flat, would have been beyond all comprehension. That's my opinion, anyway."

I smiled. "Oh, if Clayton could only hear me now! Perhaps he can. If we weren't designed for everlasting life, why would evolution have created a brain like ours with its unlimited potential? No man yet exists who can use all of the potential of his brain."

Clint laughed and told me I had a very vivid imagination when it came to consciousness.

We drove straight back to the house. Clint picked me up and carried me into the bedroom.

"I'm glad I have you for a soul mate."

"Do you really mean that?"

"Of course I do," he said in his deep husky voice.

"I think many people feel like they should be in a relationship, and they're ready to settle for any kind, as long as they're in one. Often they wind up settling for less than what they desire. It all comes back to having clarity within yourself, and knowing what you want."

"Right now," he said as he looked into my eyes. "I don't care about clarity and consciousness. All I want is your love."

A little later, I woke up feeling intensely guilty. When I was young, I used to go into the confessional at the church and confess all kinds of guilt: talking back to my parents, being unkind, having impure thoughts. Now I was feeling guilty about just one thing: not wanting to stop the monster that we had somehow created. Eventually I closed my eyes and went back to sleep.

In the dead of night, the telephone rang. I sat up straight, alarmed. "Are you going to get that?" I asked Clint.

"Yeah, I suppose," he grumbled. "On second thought, let's just let the machine take the message." He rolled over closer to the edge of the bed and turned up the volume.

"You don't listen too well, do you? I warned you once before to get off the case."

The rest of the message was garbled.

"Threats often turn out to be empty," Clint said, pretending to be unconcerned. He flicked off the machine and tried to comfort me.

"I used to think the same thing, but that was in my other life." I pulled the blankets up over my head and went back to sleep.

Weeks later, on another visit to see Uncle George, there was a new development in the case. As we were sitting at the kitchen table with him and his two nephews, one of them happened to pick up the Four Corners paper.

"Look at this!" He pointed to the front page as he handed it to Clint.

Last night, shortly before midnight, Deputy John Morgan of the Apache County Sheriff's Department was arrested after his vehicle struck a car in the parking lot of an Albuquerque bar. His blood alcohol level was at least 0.10 percent, much higher than the legal limit for intoxication in New Mexico.

This incident comes at a time when Morgan is just getting over the death of two friends who were recently killed in a bizarre accident on the Navajo reservation. The victim's relatives reported that while attending their traditional funeral ceremony, held in the Wide Ruin area on the western part of the Navajo Reservation, Morgan became frantic upon hearing that his friends' vehicle spontaneously accelerated as they approached the curve that took their lives.

"Another macabre twist to an already bizarre story."

Uncle George looked out the window at the gray sky. "They have sown the wind, and they have now reaped the whirlwind."

CHAPTER VII

It was Christmas time, and I was looking forward to the holidays. It had always meant so much to me to have my children and their families visit—especially since Clayton was gone.

I had already sent a gift to Pablo. In keeping with Spanish tradition, he and his family would celebrate the feast of Our Lady of Guadalupe, complete with Mexican food, music, dance, and culture.

The feast, especially significant to indigenous people, honored the church's first Indian saint, Juan Diego, who believers said had witnessed a dark-skinned Virgin Mary on Tepeyac hill near Mexico City in 1531. Mexican Catholics still believed in the original cast of Jesus, Mary, and Joseph, as well as the wise men and the animals.

Thinking about Pablo, I wondered if people who celebrated the typical American Christmas might reconsider whether they really wished to engage in things that captured so much attention and cost so much money.

Would that "real spirit of Christmas," which so many people speak of, be better celebrated with a selfless gift or two to someone who really needs it? Instead of buying electronic games, computer gadgets, and other gizmos, could a Christmas to remember consist of family members taking several days away from the chaos the holidays have created? How about just spending time with family, sharing stories of Christmases past with a new generation?

Who was I kidding? I loved the original idea of Christmas. I had come to detest the way the holiday had changed since I was growing up. My mother was fortunate to get a few nuts and perhaps a doll and an orange in her stocking! And she had been *thrilled*.

After we'd returned from the reservation and parked the jeep safely in our driveway, I opened the passenger door and ran ahead of Clint into the house. I immediately picked up the phone and called Connor in Colorado.

"You can't make it? Oh, I see," I said despondently as he told me that he and his wife were going to Seattle for the holidays.

"I'm so sorry, Mom."

Next I called Preston in Phoenix.

"We're taking the kids to Michigan to see Jennifer's folks. Her mother hasn't even seen our second baby, and there's already another one on the way. I'm sorry, Mom."

"I'm sorry, too."

I turned to Clint. "Trying to get my kids to visit Cornflower Corners can be quite taxing. Sometime, I think it's just too much to wish for."

"That's what happens when you have an extended family. Shall we go back to Mexico for a bit?" Clint asked.

"That would be lovely," I said, clutching his hand. "I can almost feel the ocean breezes. What about Mother?"

"She can go with us."

I picked up the phone and called her. "We're home!" I announced.

"I'm glad," she replied. "These two dogs of yours have been driving me crazy!"

"Oh, I completely forgot about the dogs."

I looked over at Clint.

"They can go, too."

"Mother, how would you like to spend Christmas in Puerto Vallarta?"

"Thanks, but I believe I'll get more rest here. You two go ahead and have a good time. Don't worry about me. I'll be fine."

I hung up and looked at Clint.

"It won't take me long to pack. After all that's happened, it will be good to get out of here," I said.

That same day we drove to the Phoenix airport. As we stood on the tarmac getting ready to board Clint's plane, I suddenly had a funny feeling. I couldn't explain it. Maybe I was still hexed.

"Are you ready?" Clint asked.

"I guess so," I said with gnawing uncertainty.

Clint started the engines. Once we were in the air, he took a quick flyby over the airport and then set course for Puerto Vallarta. The dogs and I slept most of the way.

"We're almost there." I felt Clint's hand on my shoulder as he shook me awake sometime later.

"That was a pleasant flight," I yawned.

"You were great company!" he joked.

In more serious matters, Clint had reported a loss of power several miles north of Puerto Vallarta's international airport, where he'd hoped to land. We were in the traffic pattern when I overheard the conversation between the controller and Clint.

"Sounds like you're having true mechanical problems," the controller said.

A few minutes later, the tower called back and told Clint to proceed to the airport. The next thing I knew, Clint was declaring an emergency. As per standard procedure, the tower told Clint he was clear to land on the airport's runway and that other aircraft were being kept away.

But Clint's Piper Cherokee continued to lose altitude as he made the final approach to the runway from the north. Before I even grasped the severity of our situation, it was too late.

"It's going to be close!" Clint shouted.

"I had a bad premonition about this flight…" I wanted to say. "I believe we have spiritual powers that keep us from harm," I responded instead.

"It'll take a miracle, so you'd better pray for some celestial intervention right about now," he said as he tightened his grip on the steering column.

We came within a hundred feet of crashing into the ocean.

"Do you get the impression that negativity seems to follow in our footsteps?" I asked, glancing at the emergency crews that were waiting for us. I was just about at the breaking point. "This horrifying experience isn't simply bad spirits. The root of the problem is still in the curse."

"I thought that issue was behind us?"

"Apparently not."

When we arrived at our little casa on the ocean, I looked at my watch. It was already 7:30 p.m. I flipped on the light by the back door, but it didn't come on.

"Don't panic," Clint said. "It's probably just a burned-out light bulb."

"Maybe, but I know one thing," I said shakily. "I am *not* going in there unless you turn on the lights!"

Clint went ahead of me.

"You had better take the dogs with you," I suggested as they followed him, with me right behind.

"I bet you guys are hungry!" I said as we stood in the kitchen. I glanced out the window and began to shudder. "Clint, I don't remember leaving that window open."

"I didn't forget to close it, either. Somebody's been in here. Or is *still* in here."

Suddenly the temperature in the room turned freezing cold. I began to hear the sound of wailing spirits.

"Oh, no!" I squeezed my eyes shut.

"It's all right," Clint said. "I think they're trying to warn us about approaching danger. You stay here with the dogs. I'm going to go get my gun."

"No way!" I said. "I'm not staying here alone."

Clint and I started down the hallway. After we got to the bedroom, he reached up onto the top shelf of the closet and grabbed his gun. We methodically checked out the rest of the house, looking under the beds, behind shower curtains, in the closets, and around every nook and cranny. There was no sign of disturbance anywhere. When we went back to the bedroom, I began to breathe a little easier.

"Is there anything I can get you?" Clint asked.

"Actually, there is. I would like my warm, fluffy robe."

"Where is it?"

"It's in my suitcase next to the back door."

"Okay. I'll be right back."

While he was gone, I drew some water for a hot bath. *This is going to feel good*, I thought in anticipation. Just as I was about to get in, Clint came bursting back into the room.

"Put your clothes back on. Quick! We're getting out of here."

"Why?"

"When I was in the kitchen, I smelled propane."

"Do you think there's a leak?"

"I don't know, but I'm not going to take any chances finding out. I just turned off the gas valve."

We made our way to a first-class hotel. When I saw the sunken, oval tub, I began to drool. "Maybe I'm going to get my bath yet!"

The next day, a utility repairman worked on what appeared to be a broken line. "You're very fortunate. A leak like this could have killed you."

Another brush with death, I thought. *When is our luck going to run out?*

That evening we sat out on the patio and feasted on grilled shrimp.

"I'm stuffed!" I looked up after dipping the last morsel into my cocktail sauce. "My, that was good! I hate to eat and go right to bed, but I'm exhausted. I hope tonight we can get some sleep."

As I lay in bed listening to the dogs bark at the moon, I had an eerie feeling. "Tone it down a bit!" I yelled to the dogs as I began to have a dream of hooded forms cloaked in black.

"Your vision has brought you to where you are today," a voice said.

My mind began to unveil a portrait of my brother.

"Did you say something, Clint?"

"No," he muttered.

I was finally managing to dose off when a familiar voice and the smell of smoke awakened me.

"Wake up, Sarah."

Every once in a while, just like a guardian angel, my brother would come to me in my dreams and warn me of imminent danger.

"Clint, get up. The house is on fire!"

He was already on his feet. "I can see that!"

We heard terrible screams coming from the kitchen. As we approached, I saw the door was barricaded from our side.

"I wonder who could have done this?"

"Evidently the *Chindi* believe in divine justice."

Clint smiled over at me.

"Let me out of here!" the man screamed.

"It serves you right, you bastard!"

Clint ignored his frantic pleas to open the door.

"You're not going to let him suffer like that, are you?" I said it loud enough so that the man in the kitchen would be aware of the uncertainty of his ultimate fate.

Clint moved away from the doorway. "I think we're just going to let him burn."

"No!" the man yelled, frantic.

I had a sudden change of heart. "Clint," I pleaded, "you've got to save him!"

"Let me see if I have this right. You want me to go into that burning room, with all those flames, and *rescue* him?"

"Yes! We can't just let him die."

Clint pushed away the credenza that was blocking the door. "Stand back," he cautioned. "This room is liable to implode."

The door blew open. Illuminated in the fiery glare, a hideous creature stood engulfed in flames. I clearly saw the image of the devil, the *Chindi*. Beneath a painted headdress, its vicious, massive-jowled face grimaced monstrously. So monstrously, in fact, that it reminded me of John Morgan. Spiked tusks resembling devil horns protruded from the gaping maw. Like a tortured wild animal, it howled in terror while retreating into a fetal position.

"There's nowhere you can hide, you lily-livered coward," I cursed.

As the fire shot through the crouching figure, charring it black, I smelled the odor of whiskey. Then I saw what appeared to be a long-tailed serpent coiling around the headdress. My mind flashed back to the four-hooded forms that also had infiltrated my dreams.

"Surely this can't be happening! This unearthly abomination has to be an apparition. I've never seen anything like this!" I screamed in disbelief.

The acrid odor of smoke sullied the room. I heard the terrifying sound of a man gasping, and I took a hasty step back.

What followed was even stranger. The monster's eyes began to glow an eerie red color. I had seen that exact same ruby-red tint in the *Chindi's* eyes. It seemed if it was reflecting from a torch, just before we found Juanita was dead. I tried not to think about the events of that terrible night.

Although the smoke may have obscured my vision, I could have sworn that the figure before me transformed into John Morgan. It rose on his hindquarters, wriggling and squealing like a pig.

"Is this another nightmare?" I shouted to Clint.

The stench of Morgan's burned hair and flesh filled my nostrils. His face was unreadable in the dim light, which cast a menacing shadow over his bristly jaw. Through the mystery of mental telepathy, I could somehow read what was in his mind. I could also feel the inner conflict in his thoughts. Apparently, Morgan hadn't lost his taste for murder.

The dark figure snarled at me. "You bitch! You wouldn't let me die!" His face expressed pure hatred. "I swear I'll come back. Believe me! Trust what I say. I will come back!"

"When *hell* freezes over," I replied in a hard voice.

Only seconds had passed since the door had blown open. Suddenly I felt Clint's arms tighten protectively around me. Morgan lunged at him, and a scuffle broke out. Morgan fought like the demon he was. A lingering burst of fire briefly filled the room with a flash of orange light, illuminating both men as they fell.

Morgan rolled off Clint and onto the floor. Getting to his hands and knees, he swiftly crawled on all fours down the tiled hallway.

Fear quickened my pulse. I ran back and grabbed the gun that Clint had left sitting on the hall table.

"Stop right now, or I'll shoot!" I shouted, raising the loaded revolver.

Standing up, Morgan staggered backward.

He swore and lunged again, catching me by one arm in a painful grasp that almost brought me down. As he fell, his other hand caught the material of my nightgown. I heard it rip at the waist seam.

Pure instinct made me tighten my grasp on the gun I still held between my hands. I lifted it and brought it down blindly. I had hoped to strike his head, but he was taller than I recalled. I felt a crunch as the gun hit his jaw. His pain and rage galvanized me.

I dropped the gun from my nervous fingers with a clank. I turned and fled, my feet skidding on the slippery tiled flooring as I stumbled over my trailing nightgown.

Clint, having recovered, caught Morgan in a stranglehold, but somehow he managed to break loose. A hoof-like appendage tugged at my gown as Morgan fell to the floor. A shudder rippled through my body at the sight. This nightmare was actually real.

"But you know about nightmares, don't you?" I screamed at Morgan. "You know all about death and destruction and fire!"

He went very still. "How do you know that?"

"You told me," I said bluntly. "I can read your mind."

In the next instant, I saw a tiny infant hovering above Morgan. Its doomed spirit had been cast into the outer fringes of spiritual darkness because of its father's wicked deeds. Grateful eyes touched my soul as a tiny voice thanked me.

"To walk with the creator is to truly walk in beauty. My suffering is over."

With this vision of hope, the baby was now released from its purgatory. Was this the end of the curse? Was John Morgan the baby's father and murderer? As much as my heart wished it wasn't true, and as much as I didn't want to believe it, I was becoming more and more convinced.

Suddenly the *Chindi* rose out of Morgan's body and disappeared in a swirling flash of bright flames and smoke. From the floor, Morgan looked up at me through his singed eyebrows. "Please don't let me die," he begged. His charred body looked as though it had been in an inferno.

"That's what happens when you do business with the devil. It eventually catches up with you and you have to pay the price."

In a matter of seconds, Morgan had morphed from being possessed by a demon to a worn and defeated man. He finally collapsed in a crumpled heap.

What a night. What would've become of me if Clint hadn't been there to rescue me from this nightmare straight out of hell?

He came up behind me and handed me the cell phone that was in his pocket. "Call the fire department and the police. I'll see if I can put out the fire before it does much more damage."

The next day was Christmas. There was a blurb in the Puerto Vallarta paper:

Last night, in the home of Clint and Sarah Walkerman, a flash fire almost claimed the life of Deputy John Morgan, an officer of the Apache County Sheriff's Department in Arizona, U.S.A.

Although the exact cause of the blaze has not been determined, authorities said the fire started in the kitchen of the five-bedroom home about midnight. John Morgan, the man accused of setting the fire, was apparently locked in the room where the fire started.

He is currently being closely guarded in the hospital for various charges, including arson and attempted murder. He is also being questioned and detained on an unrelated incident that happened on the Navajo Reservation eight years ago. In that case, he also possibly faces charges of murder.

Finally! Destiny fulfilled!

Later that morning, I started to write. "A fitting end to the misery. Everything is as it should be. My only regret is that Morgan still lives."

Suddenly I felt a presence all around me.

"You did the right thing." I heard my brother say.

Once again, disturbing images crept into my mind. I knew they were evil, but were they killers? I vowed that Morgan would get his due.

Emotionally drained, I bowed my head in silent prayer. It was as if a tremendous weight had been lifted from my shoulders. I never felt closer to God than I did at that moment.

Unexpectedly, the doorbell rang. I swung around in my chair and peeked out the window. When I saw my two sons with their wives standing in the alcove holding their children, along with the rest of my family, I was amazed. I could never have dreamed of receiving such a present on Christmas Day.

I ran to the door. "Come quick, Clint! We have company."

When I opened the door, Preston said, "Mom, Christmas just wouldn't be the same without you, so we decided to change our plans and bring Christmas to you and Clint."

Later on, when I had a moment to myself, I picked up my pen and wrote. "In case you were wondering, Clayton, I have learned something important: It's true. God *does* answer prayers."

The joy of Christmas carried us through spring and summer, which passed without incident. How was I to know that my peaceful tranquility would be short-lived? After months of contentment, our lives were about to change again.

Chapter VIII

"It's the end of summer, with the monsoon season already upon us, and the temperature is still over 100 degrees! Why aren't we vacationing in the Caribbean or the Mediterranean? Instead, we're stuck here, sweating it out in this miserable heat! At least in those places we could be playing on the beach and suffering in style." I looked at my husband for a reaction, but all he did was smile and nod.

"Well, things *could* be worse," I decided. "We could be shoveling coal down in Hades, for example. But even in the bowels of hell, there's got to be some relief."

After my brother's death, my mother had developed chronic lymphocytic leukemia. Her oncologist had informed her eight years ago that she had less than six months to live. She was still hanging on, and we were still counting.

When we first heard the news, we took a trip to Puerto Vallarta. The following year, we took a tour of Maui in the Hawaiian Islands.

Clint looked over at me with a concerned look on his face. "If we were to take a vacation, do you think your mother could manage on her own?"

"We should know the answer to that question soon. She's at the doctor's office right now."

"Would you like me to fix us a tropical cocktail?" he asked. "I'll even put a little umbrella in it so that we can pretend that we're in the tropics."

I nodded. "Just a small one. But don't think it will pacify me."

"I didn't think it would."

Clint walked over to the kitchen counter and fixed two exotic-looking concoctions made out of fruit juices. He garnished the glasses with fresh fruit and paper umbrellas. He came back, handed me my drink, and sank down on the sofa beside me.

The sound of the key turning in the lock of the front door caused me to rise to my feet and put my glass down on the table.

"That will be Mother," I said.

She walked across the hall briskly and stood in the doorway. Looking at the two of us, she raised her eyebrows in an expression of astonishment and slight amusement. "Guess what? My doctor says the cancer is in remission again."

"That's great news!" Clint said. "And definitely cause for a celebration."

"I agree." She came further into the room and looked at the cocktail glasses. "It appears that you two have already been celebrating," she said lightly.

Clint assured her that our beverages were nonalcoholic.

"Shall we have lunch in Scottsdale today?" I asked, still feeling elated at her news.

"That would be lovely," she answered. "There are so many good restaurants there, not like here in Cornflower Corners."

"Would you care to join us, Clint?" I asked.

"No thanks, Sarah," he replied. "I have too much work to do here at the ranch."

"Suit yourself." After searching through my purse, I found the keys to Mother's Lexus, sure she wouldn't want to ride in our jeep.

We drove past the shops on Fifth Avenue in Old Scottsdale and pulled into the parking lot of what looked like a Victorian cottage. We walked through the courtyard and past the fountain to the large beveled-glass door. A thin, dark-skinned man with quick steps opened the door and stepped back.

"*Bonjour*, ladies. Come in," he invited. "Welcome to the Fireside Inn."

We sat down at a table next to a stained glass window.

Mother sat straight in her chair, fanning herself with a lacy fan. Her eyes caught the gleam from the old-fashioned lantern on the wall. In the corner of the room was a white antique fireplace. Displayed on the mantle were several cut-glass vases brimming with flowers. Mother's eyes moved slowly around the room, taking in the charm that surrounded her.

"This is such a cheerful place. I just love everything about it: the charm, the antiquity, those flowers!" she said with a sigh.

The room in which we sat was comfortable and familiar to us. Nothing had changed in ten years. We had enjoyed many luncheons and dinners in this cozy little jewel of a restaurant, where the cuisine and ambience were decidedly not western.

The incredibly delicious food made a statement. Even their version of meatloaf had a distinctive touch. At eighteen dollars, it should! Everything appeared the same, except the prices. I was shocked.

The waiter turned to Mother. "You look lovely today, *madame*," he said with a flirtatious grin. "That's a striking jacket you're wearing."

"That's an interesting jacket you're wearing, too," Mother countered. She was probably wondering what kind of tip he had in mind. "Not everyone dons an outfit like that," she said with a sad shake of her head.

In my confusion and still suffering from price shock, I couldn't believe the scene before my eyes. This man was wearing a formal waistcoat. I'd never expected to see *this*. What were they trying to do? Trying to bring some culture to Scottsdale?

Then I heard voices coming from the kitchen. *They were speaking French!*

I listened to the bantering behind the walls. "What's going on in there?"

The waiter said nothing. He did, however, give me a grimace, as if to say, "Beats me!" Then he inclined his head and left the room in a few short strides.

Man, was I hungry! My breakfast of fruit juice just hadn't been enough. If I could only emulate my mother's well-bred silence, her quiet peacefulness… and patience.

"When are we going to eat?" I blurted out instead. I refrained from adding I was so hungry that I could eat my shoes.

"Where *is* that waiter?" I grumbled. "I still don't understand what's taking so long."

The door from the kitchen opened and he passed by us with a tray.

"*Pardon*, ladies. I'll be right with you," he exclaimed in a French accent.

Insisting that we eat something while we waited, he set a basket of rolls and butter before us. I felt faint with relief. A warm, tantalizing odor wafted out from the kitchen.

"I'm going to have the Chef's Special, *boeuf bourguignon*. How about you, Mother?"

"I have to think about it."

The waiter finally returned, and I ordered for the both of us. Two *boeuf bourguignon* and two salads. If I wanted dessert later, I could always unhook the top button of my jeans.

"Will you be having any wine with your lunch today, *madame*?" The waiter tilted his head toward mother with a glint in his eye.

"*Oui, monsieur.*"

"How about you, *mademoiselle*? You look as if you could use a glass of wine. I know *I* could," he added with a grin.

While chatting, we learned that he was some sort of a wine connoisseur. He recommended the 1996 La Poussie Sancerre Rouge from France. Then he freely admitted to sneaking a nip now and then, on the job, no less.

"I'd better go get the wine list," he said, and went back into the kitchen.

When he returned, he set two long-stemmed goblets down on the table. He smiled slightly, then mentioned that his favorite Cabernet was the Cháteau Calon-Ségur from Bordeaux.

"This is going to have to be quick," I said. He seemed ready to recite the entire wine list.

"Perhaps you would like to try one of our select wines today?" he urged.

"No, thank you. Just bring us a carafe of the house Cabernet Sauvignon."

He pranced out of the room and disappeared.

What was with this guy? Was he actually for real?

"May I offer to pour your wine for you, *madame*?" He leaned over Mother when he returned.

"*Oui, monsieur.*"

"Allow me, *madame*."

He put a napkin on his arm and poured the wine from the carafe into her glass, filling it to the brim.

That's a faux pas, right there, I thought, but let it go.

"*Merci.*"

Next the waiter poured me my glass. "Ah, this heat, it is terrible, no?" He stood there fanning himself with a napkin. "I sometimes wonder if I will ever see my home again. Such gay days we had in Paris! Not like this awful heat."

"You're from Paris?" Mother said, perking up.

"*Oui, madame.*"

A mixture of French and English words rolled off her tongue. It felt like we were in a French Bistro.

"I want you to know that Mother rarely speaks French or drinks wine unless she's celebrating a truly joyous occasion."

Catching the party mood, the waiter raised the carafe as if it were his glass. "To our two lovely *mesdemoiselles*!"

"*Mais oui*, but of course!" Mother said.

He stepped behind the server's station and promptly poured himself a glass of wine. *Probably not his first of the day*, I thought. He took a healthy gulp. I eyed him silently, my expression becoming quizzical.

"What do you think you're doing?"

"I'm having a glass of wine," he replied, tossing his head sharply with an air of importance. "You see, my *chérie*, I am not only the waiter in this establishment; I am the maître d' as well."

In my exasperation, a crude laugh bubbled up in me. I choked it back and humored him.

"Oh, really?"

He lifted his wine to toast me. "Is that a new hairstyle, *mademoiselle*? I swear you look exactly like Mary Tyler Moore."

"Why, thank you. Funny you should say that. I've been told that before!"

"Or is it Phyllis Diller I am thinking of?" he asked with a wink.

Eyes flashing, I stared at him. "By the way, *monsieur,* I like your hairstyle, too. Not everyone can wear their hair spiked like you do."

At first glance, it looked as though he had plugged his finger into a light socket.

"That's an exquisite silk blouse you're wearing," he slurred. "It brings out the highlights in your gray hair."

Mother rolled her eyes, struggling to keep from laughing. I could not prevent myself from gritting my teeth in irritation.

"My hair isn't gray. It's *frosted*! Maître d' or not, do you realize that drinking on the job is a serious matter? And no more sarcastic compliments," I demanded.

"Yes. Bon appétit!" He looked at me and then back at Mother, his smile as broad as a drunken Cheshire cat's.

"What the heck, I know you're kidding and we *are* having a celebration," I shrugged. The waiter, Mother and I all raised our glasses in a toast. "*Bonne santé*!"

Throughout lunch, Mother outwardly displayed the elation that she felt. She was in a deliriously happy frame of mind because her cancer was in remission. So was I. God forbid anything would ever happen to her. I didn't know what I'd do.

"Are you ready for another glass of wine, *madame*?"

"*Non, non*," Mother said, laughing. He caught her hand and brought it to his lips instead. "*Adieu, madame*," he murmured. "I hope that you come back soon."

Tongue in cheek, we bid "*adieu*" to the waiter *and* to the Fireside Inn. We got back in the car, and for the next half hour or so, Mother and I reminisced about old times. As we drove through the town, I caught site of an old adobe structure nestled on a hillside overlooking Phoenix. It reminded me of a home I once shared with my former husband.

Many years ago we'd had a home on the south slope of Camelback Mountain. My brother Clayton had stayed with us for several months while we'd remodeled it. I remembered him planting one hundred and twenty tomato plants in the walled-in courtyard, not realizing that the temperature inside the courtyard also reached one hundred and twenty degrees. "Anyone like stewed tomatoes on the vine?" he'd quipped as Mother and I rolled over laughing.

Clint was standing in the kitchen when I walked in.

"How was your lunch?"

"Great!" I responded. "Except for the nutty waiter we met at the Fireside Inn. Do you think I look like Mary Tyler Moore?"

"Why do you ask?"

"Never mind." I reached for the stack of mail that was on the kitchen table. "Oh, look. Here's a postcard from Conner." When I saw the golden beaches of the French Riviera displayed on the front of the card, I began to drool. My mind whirled with possibilities.

"I'm really thinking about a vacation. We need some time off. Maybe a respite on the ocean or even a sabbatical on the French Riviera. We could always fly over to Nice and join Conner for some Crêpe Suzette!"

"Forget the Rivera! I don't mind going on a short trip, but in this dead heat I'm not inclined to stray far from home. If it's all the same to you, we could go up to the old trading post again. You always liked the Navajo Reservation. Besides, it's cooler up there."

"That's not exactly what I had in mind. Maybe *you'd* like to see that creepy old place, but I don't care if I ever see it again," I replied.

"So, where do you want to go then? I'm open to ideas," Clint said.

"Any place but the trading post. Just the thought of it gives me shivers," I grimaced.

"Come on. A little road trip will do you good," he coaxed.

"Okay," I nodded. "Just keep in mind, if it's anything like our other trips, we'd be better off in hell!"

The next day I was going through my clothes, deciding what I should pack for our trip to the reservation, when Clint came into the room to find me.

"Man! It's hot today. It must be ninety-eight degrees in the shade. Hurry up! Let's get going!"

I threw the remaining clothes in my suitcase, and we left.

He was right. It *was* hot outside. We could've received third-degree burns just opening the door to the jeep. At this rate, it was going to be a long, hot summer.

It wasn't hot enough to make valley roads soft like fresh-baked cookie dough. Not yet, anyway. But it *was* hot enough to conclude that the mercury was picking up speed in its yearly climb to a hundred and ten degrees. I remembered one summer when the temperature climbed to a hundred and twenty-two degrees. Even the airplanes couldn't fly.

I was apprehensive and unsure of what to expect once we arrived at my brother's old trading post. That's where my story had first begun...

He was killed in 1992, but it seemed like yesterday. A murder is not easy to forget, especially when it's your brother. I never knew for sure who had done it and what their motive had been. Until I had some answers, I wouldn't be able to let it go.

As we drove, I noticed that the spring rains had come at the right time this year. They had encouraged the beautiful native wildflowers to bloom in the valley and also in Cornflower Corners, which was a little higher in elevation.

One of the showiest displays was at the old cemetery. It was awash with color—the glowing yellow of ragwort, the fiery color of paintbrush, and the occasional spot of vibrant blue larkspur. Soon they would begin to wilt and turn to seed. It was fitting that these native plants had found refuge here. Like the weathered headstones, they persevered.

Three hours into our trip north, we found ourselves in a hailstorm.

I looked over at Clint. "Isn't this unusual?"

"It sure is. The long-term forecast calls for hotter, dryer weather before the season ends, typically with autumn's first snowfall. I never expected this."

Since we couldn't even see the lines on the roadway, we left the interstate the first chance we got. The nearest town had one gas station, two restaurants, and a motel with its own small café. We waited with other stranded motorists for the weather to clear. Unfortunately, it just got worse.

"I have to admit it; this doesn't seem like such a great idea now," Clint remarked sheepishly. "It looks like we're going to be stuck here overnight."

The motel, with its thick-beamed ceilings, reminded me of my brother's old trading post—the place where he was killed. Someday it would be razed and go the way of other historic buildings. I used to love old buildings, but that was before my brother was murdered in a century-old compound on the reservation.

Not much had happened since the day the Mexican police had hand-cuffed the alleged suspect and transported him to the police station. I never thought that a police officer would be arrested for my brother's murder. Then again, who would know how to get away with murder better than a cop?

I wondered how Deputy John Morgan was doing. I pictured the filth in his cell and envisioned the rats crawling all over the concrete floor of the Mexican jail. Speculating about it definitely made me feel better. It was funny how fate worked out. Now it was *his* turn to suffer.

"Clint, have you heard anything from Ranger Estes about Deputy Morgan?"

"No, Sarah, although I placed a call to him a few days ago. I waited for him to return my call, but apparently I missed it. I did get a nice phone message from him, though, saying how much he enjoyed working with us. I'll call him again when we get back."

While Clint was busy signing the check-in slip, I looked around the room. "We could rent a video," I suggested with a smile, glancing at the old-fashioned rack that was hanging on the wall in the lobby. "This could actually be more fun than it seems!"

After selecting two very outdated videos, we walked over to our room. While Clint ordered room service, I decided to see if the motel had the local paper...

"Clint! You won't believe this." I came tearing back into the room. "I saw it, I read it, and read it again, but I can still hardly believe it's true," I said in a panic. "Deputy Morgan has escaped!"

"Let me see that!" Clint took the paper from my hand.

Ex-Lawman Charged with Arson and Attempted Murder Escapes Jail.

"How the hell did he manage that?"

"The former lawman, who is also wanted in the U.S. for questioning regarding the 1992 murder of a white man on the Navajo Indian Reservation, escaped from a Puerto Vallarta jail on Friday morning by beating two jailers and jumping out of a second-story window.

"Police caught a second man who had also tried to escape. Authorities became aware of the jailbreak when officers saw a suspected drug smuggler, wearing standard-issue jailhouse garb, writhing on the ground outside. He had broken his leg when the two jumped from a window, about six p.m. Friday.

"The men used their fists to beat two jailers, one male and one female, as they were being served dinner. A hospital spokesperson has said that one of the jailers was in fair condition and the other had been treated and released. Deputy John Morgan of the Apache County Sheriff's Office is still at large."

"Doesn't that sound just like him? He's accustomed to using brute force, even on tiny, helpless babies." I suddenly remembered what the medicine man had told me. "Maybe he *did* kill that baby!"

I sat for a moment, stunned.

"Don't worry, he won't get far. And I'm *not* going to allow this to spoil our camping trip." He set the paper aside. "While you were gone, I took the liberty of ordering a smorgasbord of food, which should be arriving shortly. I even ordered a bowl of freshly cooked popcorn to nibble on. I've noticed you've become somewhat of a popcorn junkie when watching movies lately."

"You're so sweet," I said, just as I heard a knock on the door. When I opened it, I couldn't believe my eyes. The waiter was holding a huge tray in his arms stacked with all kinds of delicacies, including cherrystone clams, baked crab cakes, and big shrimp. It was like dining at a coastal restaurant. Distracted by the food, Morgan faded from my thoughts.

"This is marvelous," I said, watching the waiter place the tray in the middle of the bed. "It's like being on a picnic, only better. The only thing missing is the sand."

For the next half hour or so, we gorged ourselves on the scrumptious morsels of seafood.

"Where do you suppose they get all this stuff?" I asked, popping the last clam into my mouth.

"Who knows? Maybe the owner went on a seafood junket. Now, which movie would you like to watch?" Clint asked. "You have two choices: *Misery*, the one with James Caan, where he gets stranded in a snowstorm and ends up being rescued by some whacko who abuses him, or *The Shining*."

I smiled. "The first one sounds good to me. I especially like the part where she nurses him back to health; and then, when he tries to leave, she takes a baseball bat to his legs."

"You would. I think you've always wanted to play the part of the controlling temptress," Clint said. "Personally, I prefer the idea that she seduces him with her nurturing and *then* holds him captive."

"Isn't that what I just said?" I laughed.

He jeered comically.

"I don't know what crazy fantasies are going through your head. Don't get any weird ideas," I warned.

He looked over at me with lust in his eyes. "I was just going to suggest that we turn out the lights…"

Much later we both fell asleep with the TV on.

The next morning, we packed up and checked out. Then we stopped at the nearest gas station for coffee. "You'd better go grab a few snacks," Clint suggested. "There aren't any restaurants on the way."

"You're right." I started gathering up some of my favorite goodies: three jelly donuts, two large pretzels, and a handful of assorted candies.

"What sort of culinary delights have we here?" Clint peered into the bag. "A nutritionist, she's not," he mumbled.

I looked over at him as we got back into the jeep. "I confess: I may not be the most health-conscious person in the world, but at least I don't have any known health issues."

While we devoured our donuts and pretzels, we navigated the flat stretches of high desert highways. "Let's not miss the McGinnis signpost," I cautioned, as we approached the reservation. I remembered when I had missed it before, but I would never tell Clint that. Like my brother, he would have never let me live it down.

"How could we miss it? It's the size of a billboard."

"It's easy to get lost around here," I said in my own defense. "Then again, *I* could get lost just about anywhere. It's a special talent of mine. I remember when I was visiting Tokyo and I took the bullet train...It took me two days to find my way back. The airline I worked for wasn't very pleased."

"Did you forget, I'm Navajo? I know this country like the back of my hand."

"There it is!" I yelled. "It sure could use a fresh coat of paint."

As we turned off the highway, it felt as though we were being lured into a mystical foreign land. It was like leaving one world and entering another. Conical peaks of white granite alternated with striking formations of boulders. The views of the surrounding mountains swept out for miles. The plant life, which included everything from spiky ocotillo bushes to tall agaves with creamy colored stalks, framed a pristine horizon of starkly angled hills.

We drove along the sheep trails and through the arroyos. We decided to take the back way up to the trading post rather than navigate the steep hill. Beginning at the creek bed, we quickly made a run up the slope, actually cresting at the top.

We parked the jeep in the yard and walked over to the trading post.

My first inkling that something was wrong occurred when I approached the front door. Several rattlesnakes lay coiled on the ground, their tails rattling and their tongues hissing. I gasped in horror. The snakes were *far* too close for comfort.

"Get out of here, you little bastards!" Clint yelled as he stomped his feet, creating vibrations.

The snakes slithered off in every direction, heading for cover in the brush.

"I'll have to try that sometime," I said as I stepped back.

Smiling, Clint looked over at me. "What makes you think you can relate to animals?"

"I've done it before," I replied heatedly.

"When?"

"A long time ago. I'll tell you all about it sometime. Right now though, I think I'm about to faint."

"You'll be all right," he said as he came over and wrapped his jacket around me.

"Easy for you to say. You didn't have five snakes almost twined around your ankles," I retorted.

"It's time to break out the camp stove!" Clint grinned.

"Don't say that. And please don't say we're spending the night, either. I've already had enough of this place. If I wanted to scare the bejeebers out of myself, I would've rented *Night of the Living Dead*.

"I'll make a note of that," Clint laughed. "But we *are* staying the night."

"Well, that movie is exactly what this place reminds me of," I continued. "At any moment, I fully expect to see a bunch of zombies popping out of the bushes."

Clint rolled out the double sleeping bag with pillows in the back of the jeep. I looked into his topaz-colored eyes and a rush of warmth flooded my body. I leaned over and kissed his cheek. "Sorry, I didn't mean to get so testy."

"That's okay. I promise I won't tease you anymore. Ah," he exclaimed, as he laid his head down on the pillow. "Just being here is so relaxing and refreshing."

"You're right." I stared out the window, watching the storm clouds float across the sky. "There's nothing like sleeping outdoors—being alone in the vast wilderness, listening to the coyotes howl, and replaying *Night of the Living Dead* in your head. It really takes you away from the everyday, humdrum world."

A concern crept into my mind as I lay there. I wondered if the curse of the *Chindi* was truly over. Were the evil spirits finally at peace? I still didn't know whether the *Chindi* were the alter ego of John Morgan. Were they really one in the same?

"I curse thee, John Morgan." The words escaped my lips. I didn't realize how those few words would resurrect the ghosts of the past. I didn't realize that this time, they would return with an even greater vengeance.

We spent the next day meandering around the old trading post. When we came to the building where my brother's body was found, I realized that it had been burned to the ground. The Indians believed that whenever a death occurred, everything around it must be destroyed in order to release the spirit.

"Whoever did this probably meant well," I said, "but they have also managed to destroy even more evidence!" I looked at Clint. "I don't know about you, but I've seen all I want to see. I'm ready to go home."

He looked surprised. "Well, if that's what you want..."

"Shall we spend the night in a motel? Or would you prefer to drive back home?" I asked. "I hate to be away too long. I'm sure the dogs are suffering from separation anxiety by now."

"Will you quit worrying about those two dogs? There's nothing—and I mean *nothing* that the two of them can't handle on their own."

"Then why didn't we bring them with us?" I asked.

"Well, I was concerned for their safety. I didn't think it would be a good idea to bring them with us, especially since the last time we were here, we encountered a gang of drug dealers and the *Chindi*."

"Exactly my point," I said.

"Jeez," he grumbled. "Give me a break. The poor things needed a little recovery time."

"And I didn't? You seem to have forgotten that we also encountered bats and a bear," I retorted. "Along with that gang of drug dealers and the *Chindi*."

"I know, but you have me to protect you," he said. "Besides, what do you plan to do if that hideous-looking creature with the painted headdress and broken teeth shows up?"

"I'll flash my bear amulet at him," I joked.

"I'm serious, Sarah. You know that in Navajo mythology, the bear is the most powerful of beasts. In the face of danger, he guards his territory with all his might. And this is his territory. Remember…he lives just below us."

"Did you have to remind me?" I sighed. "Maybe you're right. Who knows?"

I thought back to the time when I had heard the eerie wails of the *Chindi* echoing through the house in Puerto Vallarta. Now I wore my dangling bear necklace and I felt protected. I had placed my other bear necklace around Callista, my little wolf, and she was protected, too. "There are a lot of things we don't understand…"

"You know what I think, Sarah?" Clint stood with his arms around me as we looked out at the mountains. "I believe the secret tunnel cave we explored last summer is part of an interconnected system that extends throughout all of these mountain ranges."

"I never gave it a second thought. Do you think the bear considers the entire reservation his stomping grounds?" I asked.

"There's a good probability," he replied.

"That's great news!"

"Shall we go cave exploring?" he asked.

I smiled. "Not without the dogs."

"Okay, we'll go home, get the dogs, and come back."

We decided to drive to Pinetop, a nearby town.

"I bet you didn't know that the Amateur Fiddler Contest is happening here tonight." Clint looked over at me.

"You're right, I didn't. Where is it being held?"

"Just down the street."

"Let's go!"

We drove to the old-time saloon.

"That girl is good," I said, listening to her fiddle as we walked in.

"How do you know that?"

"Because my dad was a concert violinist and I was his protégé, that's how. And if you *must* know, I received a violin scholarship."

"Go get the fiddle, Ma." Clint grabbed me and we began dancing.

"This is so much fun!" I laughed as he twirled me around. "It's good to kick up your heels once in awhile!"

After a night of revelry, we checked into a nearby motel.

"You know, Clint," I said as we walked up to our room, "I'm proud to be your wife."

"I'm glad you said that," he smiled. "Nothing makes me more proud than to have you by my side."

For the remainder of the night we stayed wrapped in each other's arms.

The next morning, we drove back to Cornflower Corners. "Who would ever think, being the cosmopolitan people that we are, that we would end up in this small town?"

"It's not so bad here," Clint replied. "Although I much prefer our home in Puerto Vallarta, mostly because it's on the beach."

"When are we going back?"

"Did you forget our plane is still in the shop for repairs?" He grimaced at me. "Ever since you decided to take flying lessons," he added. "Remember?"

"I didn't do anything to the plane!"

"Of course not. You just spilled a little coffee on the control panel. That's all."

"I'm sorry!"

"Things could have been worse. A *lot* worse," he commented. "I've seen your flying ability, after all."

"I guess you're right," I replied, remembering the time I had neglected to bank the plane in a turn.

"You'd better leave the flying to me," Clint chuckled. "Just watching you drive the jeep is bad enough!"

"That's enough bashing."

"You're right." He leaned over and kissed me.

"That's better."

When we arrived home, the dogs greeted us warmly, and so did my mother. She always dreaded when we left her with the obligation of caring for them. They were definitely a handful.

"Guess what, Mother? We're going back up to the reservation tomorrow."

"Oh, no."

"Don't worry. We're taking the dogs with us."

"Thank God!" she said under her breath. "What time are you planning to leave?"

"I don't know. Probably as soon as we can get ready."

"What do you find so fascinating about that reservation, anyway?"

"Clint thinks the underground caves we stumbled upon last summer extend throughout all of the mountain ranges."

"So?"

"So, we're going exploring. Who knows what we'll find."

"You two are crazy. I just hope you don't meet up with that bear again."

"Didn't you know? The bear is our protector!"

She just shook her head.

I spent most of the day tending to chores, and then I started packing.

"You might want to bring a pad and pencil." Clint smiled over at me. "I have a feeling this is going to be the last part of your book, in a possible series of books."

"Writing a sequel should be a little easier. Fortunately my two sons convinced me to replace my old word processor with a new computer. I don't know how many hours I've wasted retyping, moving paragraphs around, and printing out drafts, page by page."

"Someday you'll be telling all that to Oprah," he laughed.

"Wouldn't that be something? I don't really want recognition, though. I just want to tell my stories. I remember the time when I took my kids on an overnight train ride to Durban, a town located on the coastal tip of South Africa. The gal who rode the train with us couldn't wait for me to tell the next story. My children were already asleep at that point. And she was an adult who wanted me to continue with my bedtime stories!"

"Would you tell me a bedtime story? I'm just about ready to hit the hay." He fluffed his pillow in preparation.

"Sure, but I must warn you, it could get a little scary…"

"That's all right. I'll be brave."

"You're going to have to be, because it's about a prince who rescues his princess from the imps of the netherworld. Even more entertaining than the battles between good and the evil is the part where he caters to her every whim."

"That story sounds suspiciously real." He reached over and turned out the light.

"Good night."

***

The next morning, I woke up and pulled my white cotton robe around me. Picking up my suitcase, I stumbled sleepily into the hallway, where I caught sight of two sets of pointed ears in my peripheral vision. Immediately the dogs came over to greet me. "Yes, you're going with us today," I told them. They started wagging their tails. "Now, go get your master up!"

They scampered into the bedroom. Wrangler and Callista were inseparable. It made me think about the passing of my sweet dog, Roper. He had once taken a rattlesnake bite meant for me. My dear dog was now buried beneath a paloverde tree under four feet of garden loam on a hillside by our house. He still came to me when I called him in dreams. It didn't really matter where he was buried. Like my brother, Roper would always be remembered.

After making a pot of coffee, I returned to the bedroom. Clint was sitting up in bed, glowering at the two dogs.

"Aha! I *knew* you sent them in here."

"You're right, I did. As a special favor."

"Smart aleck!"

I stood next to the bed. "Are you going to get ready for this trip? Or sit around making snide comments?"

I leaned against the bedpost, waiting for him to start moving.

"You'd make a good drill sergeant," he mumbled. "At least let me have a cup of coffee!"

We lingered longer than we should have. After loading the two dogs into the jeep, we left for the reservation.

"Shall we have breakfast in Payson?" I asked.

"Sounds good to me."

"What are we going to do with the dogs?"

"We'll just leave them in the jeep. It's not very hot up here."

We went on until we came to Main Street Payson, off Highway 87. We pulled into the gravel lot of what looked like a Countryside Inn and walked past the hitching posts to the large wooden doors. It was not open yet, so we entered through the garden gate and knocked gently at the back door. A thin, dark-skinned man opened it.

"Bonjour. Come in," he invited. "Please be seated."

"Not *you* again!" My face dropped.

The waiter grinned and clasped his hands. *"Mon chérie,"* he yelled excitedly. "You have come back to me!"

"You're blushing," Clint observed.

The waiter took me by the arm. In shock, I allowed him to escort me to the dining room.

"I see you finally found yourself a man, *mademoiselle.*" He lowered his voice. "And not a bad-looking one, at that!" He winked.

"I don't know if I'm ready for this," I muttered to myself.

He seated us at a table next to a pane glass window.

Clint gave me a wry look of sympathy over his shoulder. "Who *is* that dude?"

"He's the nutty waiter Mother and I met that time we had lunch at the Fireside Inn in Scottsdale."

"Rumor has it that place went out of business."

"I can see why."

I unfolded the morning paper. Mexico Arrests Fugitive Ex-Governor in Drug Case was the first article to capture my attention. *Federal police arrested a former official suspected of protecting drug smugglers, ending a two-year search for one of Mexico's most wanted fugitives.*

"You might want to read this along with me," I advised Clint. "It may have something to do with Morgan."

He scooted next to me and we began to read together.

Diego Hernandez was arrested while traveling in Cancún with two other people, including a former state judicial police officer. Hernandez, who faces drug smuggling and organized crime charges, is the highest-ranking Mexican official ever to face a drug investigation while in office. Authorities accused him of helping drug smugglers during his 1993–1999 administration, during which time the drug trade boomed.

The main accusation against Hernandez is that he used police to help protect drug smugglers from a group known as the Juárez organization. Hernandez has denied the allegations, saying they were motivated by political rivalries.

After being questioned by Mexico's drug czar and summoned for further testimony, Hernandez shook off a police tail and disappeared two weeks before the end of his term as governor of Quintana Roo, where Cancún is located.

Hernandez's ability to elude authorities led opposition lawmakers to charge that the Attorney General's Office had allowed him to escape to avoid further embarrassment to the governing party.

Officials have said drug trafficking grew substantially in Quintana Roo during Hernandez's administration, when former law-enforcement officials aided drug smugglers.

One of those former officials is Vincente Alcides Banderas, also known as "El Toro," who heads up the Cancún operation of the cocaine smuggling organization that grew out of the Juárez Cartel after the death of its leader in 1997. Some say Alcides Banderas, a former police official, is the world's top drug lord.

"Do you suppose this guy 'El Toro' knows anything about my brother's murder? Maybe he could lead us to the killer. He might have been part of the Juárez regime during the time he got killed."

"I don't know, but we can find out."

"Good. I've never been to Cancún."

"That's not what I meant. I'll call the office and see if Ranger Estes knows anything about this." Clint took out his cell phone.

"So you think there may have been a connection between this guy 'El Toro' and John Morgan?" Clint asked as he held it to his ear. "Interesting," he said in a cold voice.

"You were right, Sarah," Clint said as he got off the line. "This guy 'El Toro' was part of the regime that worked the Four Corners area during the time of your brother's murder. Not only that, Morgan's escape may have been rigged. According to my sources, authorities may have let him go rather than having to deal with the complex procedure of extradition. However, they believe he may have committed suicide. Talk about crooked cops."

The nosy waiter had apparently overheard us. "I don't mean to butt in," he said as he brought out our food. "But is that the same cop who blew that poor slob's head off up on the Navajo Indian Reservation?"

"Yes. That 'poor slob' was my brother."

"Please forgive me, *mademoiselle*! I didn't mean to be insensitive. My condolences!"

I picked dejectedly at my cheese omelet and pushed the hash browns around on my plate. My mind was whirling with guilt and memories.

"Is there something wrong with the food?" the waiter asked, genuinely concerned.

"No, it's fine," I replied.

The waiter did his best to be charmingly attentive. He gave us courteous service and kept a surreptitious eye on us in case we needed something or wanted the check.

"Is there anything else I can get you? Perhaps you would like some caramel pecan rolls? On the house, of course!"

"No, thank you," I said, reaching for my purse as we got ready to leave.

"Before you go, *mademoiselle*," he stopped me. "Through the grapevine in this town, I heard rumors that your brother's murder had something to do with drugs. Not that he was a drug pusher, mind you, but he knew who was and was prepared to identify them. They say that's why they shot him."

I looked at him as we stood to leave. "Believe it or not, I think you're right. But we haven't been able to prove it so far."

"It was good of you to come." The waiter kissed my hand.

"Good bye, sir." He shook Clint's hand.

As we walked to the door, I heard his voice again. "*Au revoir, mademoiselle.* I still think you look like Mary Tyler Moore!"

I gritted my teeth, looking over at Clint. "The last time I saw that waiter in Scottsdale, he accused me of looking like Phyllis Diller, a much less flattering comparison."

We got into the jeep, a full-fledged BoonDocker with a four-wheel-drive system that was rugged enough for rocky trails and refined enough for highway travel.

"Well, thank goodness it's still here!" Clint said, realizing that he had left the keys in the ignition.

"Would you try to steal a vehicle with two big watchdogs sitting in the front seat?"

"I guess not." He smiled warmly at Wrangler and Callista, who slobbered a greeting in return. "You two dogs are going to have a jouncy ride ahead."

Once we arrived in Indian territory, Clint turned toward me. "Would you like to go over to the Hopi Reservation and see a Hopi snake dance?"

"No, thanks. I've had my share of thrills with rattlesnakes. Enough to last me a lifetime, actually."

As soon as the dogs' paws hit the front yard of the trading post, they took off. "Hey, come back here!" I yelled. "There's work to do!"

Clint started dividing up our camping gear. "I hope you packed in a way that we can get at what's needed without a hassle. Not like the time you stacked all of our cooking supplies on top of our rain gear."

"Of course I did!"

"What's in this bag?" He reached in and pulled out a camera, powerful binoculars, and a big book. "Why did you bring all this stuff?" he complained peevishly. "Especially a tome like Michener's *Hawaii*. You'll never read it!"

"I think I feel a sermon coming on."

"No, just pearls of wisdom. Hikers should carry forty percent or less of their body weight, so being thrifty is important. I'm sorry, but these things are going to have to remain in the jeep."

"Yes, sir!" I saluted.

Clint gave me a slightly reproachful look and uttered a military command. "At ease, woman." Then he saluted with his hand in the prescribed position.

"Methinks this is going to be a longer than usual summer." I sighed.

While traipsing around the grounds, we stumbled upon a colony of red fire ants. It was the biggest residential colony of ants I'd ever seen, substantially larger than the ones they had in South Africa, which were humungous.

"Wouldn't it be awful to be eaten alive by them?" I cringed, watching the giant ants crawl into their giant anthill.

"It would be pretty painful. My ancestors used to tell me stories. During the wars between the Indian and the white man, when an Indian was fortunate enough to capture a white person, he would look for such an anthill. After binding his victim in wet leather, he would stake him to the ground. Then he would sprinkle granules of grains in the person's eyes, ears, nose, and mouth. It was very effective. If only I could get Morgan up here alone, I know how I'd make him talk."

"How barbaric! No wonder my mother was afraid of Indians since she saw *The Last of the Mohicans!*"

I sat down on a rock and reached for my pencil to write the reminders in my notebook.

Clint peered over my shoulder. "May I see?" he asked. "You're not writing…You're drawing a picture of a man with a boar-like face being eaten alive by a giant fire ant."

"What's your point?"

"You would probably make a better torturer than I would," he laughed.

Later that evening, in preparation for bed, we spread a foam pad on the ground and pitched a lightweight netted tarp over it in case it should rain.

Predicting the arrival of the monsoon season always seemed to be a big mystery. Only Mother Nature knew for sure when the combination of moisture and shifting winds would trigger the violent thunderstorms that subsequently led to flash floods.

I found it difficult to get to sleep that night. The wind had shifted from the north, and now was bringing in warm, moisture-laden air from the Gulf. The dark clouds had moved in. I heard the incessant croaking of the frogs celebrating the return of warmer humid weather, as well as the occasional yip-yip of a coyote, the hoot of an owl, and other, more mysterious night cries from the wildlife.

I tossed and turned beneath my mosquito net, thinking about the man lying next to me. He was truly my soul mate and friend. He was smart, sexy, and caring; all I'd ever hoped for in a man.

Then I thought about my brother, who was killed execution-style on this very property. The police were no longer searching for his murderer or seeking a motive for the killing. But *I* still was, and that's what kept bringing me back.

CHAPTER IX

The next day I was awakened by a furtive sound outside our sleeping quarters. It was not a loud sound, but it puzzled me, even in my sleep. I heard the warning chirp of a bird followed by two frightened barks from each of the dogs. Then silence. I got up and drew my jacket around me. Before walking outside, I glanced back over my shoulder at our makeshift bed.

It was empty!

Now I knew what I had heard. Clint had been moving down the slope of a hill, step by careful step, stalking his prey in anticipation of breakfast.

"Come here, little rattlesnake," I heard him say.

"I hope you don't seriously think that I'm going to eat that?" I uttered when I caught up to him.

He turned to me, just as the rattlesnake struck out at him.

"Gotcha!" He grabbed the snake just behind the head, piercing its venomous skull with his spear.

"Yikes!" It was all I could think of to say.

After breakfast, which consisted of grilled prickly pear pads, eggs and rattlesnake meat, we headed for the caves. But not before I snuck my camera into my backpack. "Clint will never know the difference," I said quietly to myself, knowing that I hated being told what to do.

"What's this?" Clint stopped short, looking at the ground. I stood beside him and stared down at the tiny bundle of bones and the broken owl's feather barely visible in the dirt below. "If I were you, I wouldn't touch that feather. According to Navajo belief, the owl represents wisdom, but it can also represent the devil and it could take you to hell."

"Too late," I said, holding it in my hand. "Do you really believe that a feather and a few pieces of bone could hurt me?"

"Surely you must remember the time when Morgan and his buddies put a small piece of bone in the cockpit panel of the plane and the plane almost went down?"

"Do you think that someone is playing voodoo tricks on us?"

"It would seem. We know one thing to be true. Morgan wants us to die."

I felt a chill. That was what voodoo was all about, after all—the belief that an enemy could wish death on someone.

The dogs found an opening behind some bushes. We slid down until we reached the bottom. Then we descended into the cave. The dogs led us to a rock wall festooned with long white mucus-like colonies of bacteria. On some walls the bacterial slime grew in phlegm balls.

"Good God! These weird-looking gooey globs look as if they belong on another planet," I said.

Just past the wall, we continued to follow the cave's passageway. It was a winding succession of galleries decorated with prehistoric art. We started naming them. The first one we came to, we called The Bat Room. Perhaps five varieties of bats were roosting on the ledges above. Species that looked as though they were extinct existed in this wretched looking cave.

"They're incredible!" I said, looking at the small reptiles and mammals. The deeper we went, the colder and drearier the cave became. Its unique life forms made it all worthwhile, though. Light streams filtered through one of about five skylights, giving that part of the cave its name. The sunlight pierced the room through the skylights, and water bubbled up from a nearby stream. As we climbed upward toward the sunlight, a stream of water trickled over a channel of rocks, and fish pooled below.

Thinking back to our discovery of the cave, I became entranced. Over in the corner was a group of giant lizards that resembled the Komodo dragon. I was suddenly terrified that one of those monsters was going to sprout wings and carry my writhing body to places unknown.

And, that's exactly what happened…

Spiraling downward through staircases made of stone, I felt myself falling. For an instant, it felt as though I had been transported to hell. There were balconies chiseled into the rock. Sticklike figures with mask-shrouded faces peered over the edges as if they were prisoners. Some staircases led to nowhere, with ropes and ladders hung in suspension. Below, murky swamps were filled with alligators…and dungeons and dragons. Those terrifying, fire-breathing beasts were enough to freak out anyone.

Plunging further into the abyss, I thought I recognized the two men who had something to do with my brother's murder. And then I saw Jerome Kramer, who'd also had a hand in it. But I couldn't find John Morgan for some reason. Then I realized that was because he wasn't dead. He was still alive.

When I came back to reality, I realized I had been transported to hell in a vision.

"Clint, you don't suppose that Morgan is hiding out in the Four Corners area, do you? He knows this country as well as you do."

"I don't know, but he has a much better chance of getting lost in Mexico than he does in the States."

"I guess you're right."

After climbing almost a hundred feet up the stone ledges, we came upon a footpath laid with stones. We followed it to an opening hewn in the rock in the shape of an archway. When we entered, we saw a passageway that led deeper into the mountain.

"I wonder if the cave has been found and explored since the time of the Anasazi…" I mused.

"It's possible," Clint admitted. "Although I don't see any remnants left by later visitors."

He turned on his heavy-duty flashlight. Only then did we venture inside. The passageway was smoothly carved from the rock and sloped downward for about fifty feet, ending in a small chamber with dozens of strange and ancient-looking petroglyphs. Clint went on to describe the hieroglyphics etched on the walls and ceiling of the chamber.

"Did they record these red symbols with some sort of natural dye?"

"No. They were etched with blood."

"What kind of blood?" I probed.

"Sometimes animal, sometimes human."

Another room was filled with artifacts. Clint flashed his light in a sweeping motion. "Someone has been here recently."

"Why do you say that?"

"Just a gut feeling," Clint said, "but I doubt anything will materialize from it."

We moved closer to the center. I could feel the heat emanating from the hearth in the middle of the room.

"And very recently, too" I added.

"We have our work cut out for us." Clint paused. "We should probably authenticate these artifacts. I'm going to call my friend, Professor Farrari. He knows a lot about archaeology and geology. He'd be very excited to see these artifacts, and he could tell us what agency should be notified."

"When my mother was a little girl she used to take piano lessons from a professor by the same name. He would always encourage her to drink a glass of wine with a raw egg in it. I wonder if they're related?"

"We'll know in a few hours. I'll let you ask him if he likes raw eggs with his wine."

Shortly after we emerged from the cave, Clint turned impatient. "Let's head back to the campsite now. We can call him on my cell phone."

We quickly made our way back.

"Are you sure you want to come up here?" Clint asked Professor Farrari.

His reply was instantaneous. "Yes, absolutely."

"All I can tell you is that based on my observations, this stuff appears to be genuine." Clint paused. "If it's not a hoax, it could very well prove to be the archaeological find of the century."

He turned to me. "Okay. We've got an expert in our camp. We should have no problem identifying the artifacts."

The professor was not what I had expected; he was a cross between Albert Einstein and Frankenstein. He had white flowing hair and I could see his bony knees protruding from his khaki pants as he climbed out of the car.

Still, I was glad he had arrived early.

"This is what you dogs have been waiting for." I picked up my backpack, threw a scarf over my shoulder, and we left.

"Lead the way," the professor offered.

We walked past the room with the gooey droopy globs. The professor turned to me. "I am not a microbiologist or someone who specializes in astrobiology or extraterrestrial life, but I am convinced that these weird-looking extreme forms of microbes could be an analog to life we might someday find deep beneath the surface of Mars."

"That's exactly what I thought," I replied. "See, I'm not the *only* one who thought so." I looked triumphantly over at Clint. He gave me a stern look in return. "Well, maybe those weren't my *exact* words," I qualified.

We reached the Skylight Room at last. Clint stood at the edge of the calm and crystal water, waiting until the professor and I caught up.

Suddenly Wrangler bounced up and dove into the water. He had a habit of diving for rocks, but brought up a small copper object in the shape of a bell instead. "How beautiful," I said, admiring the etchings.

The professor was nearly speechless. "I've never seen a dog do that trick, nor have I heard of any copper artifacts of that size. The early Indians mostly dabbled with small baubles and beads."

"We're almost to the room with the artifacts," Clint said.

"How far from here?" asked the professor.

"Ninety to a hundred yards," Clint answered, pointing. "Just around that bend in the tunnel."

Clint flashed the light in the direction we were heading. We rounded the bend, moving around the contour of the mountain and following the river. Suddenly, he thrust out his arm and abruptly stopped.

"Switch off your light!" he ordered the professor in a hushed voice. We all saw a light beyond the tunnel. I grabbed both dogs and whispered to them to be quiet.

The professor complied, casting the chamber into eerie blackness. A dim glow filtered through one of the portals and reflected off the water in front of us. "I think we have looters," Clint said.

There were two men inside the chamber working feverishly, loading artifacts into burlap bags.

"Why do these characters always take this stuff?" he demanded, noticeably agitated.

"Because it's worth money," the professor broke in. "Look at that burly guy, who's holding that magnificent sculptured head. It's priceless."

"Does that guy look like Morgan?" I asked. "Or is it just a figment of my imagination?"

"It does kind of look like John Morgan. Perhaps he has a new occupation."

What happened next shocked us all. The man holding the sculptured head set it down on a rock. As the other man bent down to retrieve another artifact, a big hairy paw knocked it out of his hands. Picking up Morgan's cohort by the head, powerful arms with knife-like claws squeezed, drawing the life out of him.

Clint drew his gun. "Hands up! You're busted!"

I reached for the camera that was in my backpack and turned on the flash. "Smile, pretty!" I said as I clicked. The next thing I knew, the man who looked like Morgan was gone, and so was the big hairy creature. The dogs started to go after the animal, but I called them back and ordered them to stay.

"What the hell was that?" asked the professor, who looked as though he had just seen the Loch Ness Monster.

"A bear that lives in these caves," Clint said matter-of-factly.

He moved forward through the narrow opening. "There's nothing we can do for him," he said as he knelt over the dead man. He rapidly groped through the man's pockets and recovered a wallet. It came as no surprise that it was empty of identification.

However, tucked inside a hidden compartment was a photograph of a beautiful woman with blue-gray eyes. Clint, mesmerized, sucked in a deep breath as his stare shifted to her pink jumpsuit. Over the finely contoured breasts was an overlay of the crosshairs of a gun with an *X* drawn through it. Shock and then grief overwhelmed him. The woman in the photo was his dead wife.

"Find what you were looking for?" asked the professor.

"Definitely more than I bargained for," Clint replied. He passed the picture to the professor. "You remember my first wife, Ariel, who took a bullet that was meant for me. This is a picture of her just before she died."

"Dare I ask what her picture would be doing in the corpse's wallet?"

"That's a good question."

I could see that Clint was stunned. I guess anything was possible, especially since the DEA employed her as an undercover agent. Clint asked me if I had a plastic bag in my backpack. I hurriedly rummaged through and found one. He placed the picture and wallet in the bag and handed it to me for safekeeping.

Suddenly we heard an explosion.

"You don't suppose that son of a bitch is trying to block our way out of here, do you?" He looked over at the professor.

"It sounds like a cave-in to me."

Just then a surge of water broke loose and came roaring through the tunnel. I grabbed the head, hastily wrapped it in my scarf, and shoved it in my backpack. It was all we were able to preserve.

Feverish with excitement, hope, and fear, I followed Clint into a long narrow corridor, the professor falling in behind. The dogs were ahead of Clint. We had only gone a few steps when we heard another explosion. At the far end, the pillars supporting the arched entrance split from top to bottom, buckling and collapsing, and an avalanche of earth and rock gushed through, blocking our escape.

"Get back!" Clint shouted above the horrendous din. "Get back before the whole tunnel caves in!"

Whimpering, I pressed my face against his chest. We all carefully retraced our way. Dogging our trail back to the chamber was a great rumbling surge of water as the tunnel sagged and broke. Shards of stone scattered around us like hail, and then whole slabs broke free from overhead and walled up what was left.

"Another good surge, and this will fall in on us, too," Clint growled, scrutinizing the debris by the feeble light of his flashlight.

"Let it," I mumbled. "It would be merciful."

"There's no way out as it stands," Clint confirmed.

Clutching him, I happened to look down and see a chute-like opening in the floor. I knelt down and frantically groped at the opening. My heart throbbed as if it would burst. "Yes, there is!"

"What? Where?"

"Down here! It's an underground river," I said, praying that it wasn't a mirage.

"Damn my eyes if you're not right!" Clint flashed his light over the thick square opening. "But it's filled with murky water." He backed away from the stench. "This is crazy," he groused. "There's nothing but muck down there."

"Perhaps not," the professor said. "The river is wide, and there's a fair chance it will lead us out of this hellish nightmare."

"A lousy chance," Clint replied, "but the only one we've got right now."

"Just think of it as a neighborhood cesspool—and let's hope it isn't too deep to drown in," the professor added.

Giving the dogs a pat on the head, Clint nudged them off the lip of the opening. Callista and Wrangler yelped and plunged feet-first down the hole, their howls ending abruptly in a dull splash of water. Clint dove a second later. I made sure my backpack was secure to my back.

"Jump!" Professor Farrari ordered me.

Shaken, I hesitated at the brink of the hole, peering down into the dark, unable to see Clint or the dogs.

"Jump!" Professor Farrari repeated.

So I did. I dropped down the opening, my eyes squeezed shut and my body coiled, ready to pull free from any creepy crawlies that lay at the bottom. My feet touched the bottom, then sank. Frantically, I tried kicking free of the clinging silt that oozed up around my knees, struggling to hold onto the backpack that had slipped off my shoulder. Then the professor was down beside me, wrenching at my free arm and breaking me from the river's murkish trap.

Following his lead, I swam through the stirred-up water, refusing to give in to my doubts and fears. *I would reach the surface*, I told myself. As long as I kept up with Clint; as long as I kept faith in him.

My lungs were beginning to ache, but I called on my inner reserves of strength. Despite my swimming ability and trust in Clint, a sensation of dread seeped through me as I forged ahead. We'd made a mistake, a fatal error, and the three of us were going to drown, trapped under the surface where nobody would ever find us.

I forced the panic down and stifled the scream welling up in my chest. I struggled to hold my breath, straining for each inch forward. There had to be an opening above, soon, there just had to be. I could not die this way. My conscious thoughts touched on the grief that would soon overcome my family.

I thought of my two sons and felt a deep sense of loss, knowing that I would not be there to see my granddaughter and my four grandsons reach maturity. And what would become of my poor mother without me?

Thinking of this, I swam with renewed strength, vowing not to leave them this way.

I finally surfaced, my head reeling and my stomach knotted with convulsions. Water lapped against my face, and I choked, gagging. It was an inky black, but still a softer black than the water had been. It allowed me to see the general shape of the chamber and a narrow stone ledge running parallel, a few feet to my right.

"Over this way!"

I turned slightly toward the sound, was able to make out Clint sitting slumped on the ledge. I swam toward him, catching the sound of splashing nearby, as well as the ragged gasp of someone sucking some much-needed air.

"Professor Farrari, is that you?" I called.

"Yeah. I'm right behind you."

Another echoing surge came, and this time Wrangler and Callista finally surfaced, making noises like beached whales. They'd somehow taken in a breath of water along the way and were suffering a spell of coughing. They trailed the professor to the slime-coated ledge, where the two men helped them out of the water.

"One more stroke and I'd have sunk for sure," I wheezed after I'd recovered enough to talk. "Now what?"

"We walk."

When we reached the safety of the camp, I removed the backpack and immediately checked to see if anything had gotten wet—but the head, the camera, the wallet and picture, and even the notepad concealed within the waterproof fabric had made it through undamaged.

"If you don't mind, I'll take that carving and turn it over to the university," the professor said, taking the head carefully from my hands. "Since we can't do anything without the rest of the artifacts, I guess I'll head for home."

"I'm going home, too," I said.

I started to walk away, only to be stopped by Clint grasping me by the arm. "Let me go, Clint! Don't you see? Morgan and his henchmen have out-maneuvered us, and this time they're using dynamite, not just voodoo like we were expecting. It's a disaster!"

"Your wife's right," the professor said, eyeing Clint sympathetically. "It's not going to get better by blindly chasing after them. The only thing you'll accomplish is your own death."

"I've got to try."

"You can't go after Morgan by yourself!" I cried.

"Hell!" Clint said, releasing his grip on my arm. "But we can't simply allow those bastards to get away with murder and destroying everything in their path."

"I don't like it any better than you do, but the damage has already been done. Your wife is dead, and so is my brother. We can't save them; we can't turn the clock back. And I'm not about to commit suicide fighting a battle that can't be won, not when I can live to defeat them another day, in some other place, in some other way."

"Yeah? Well, where and how are you going to do it, Sarah?"

"I don't know," I sighed. "Damn! If we only knew what they were planning to do next."

"I know," Clint said. He passionately launched into a concise recounting of Morgan's mode of operation and how he would most likely cross the border into New Mexico.

"Would you like me to drop the dogs off at your place?" the professor asked.

"That would be great." Clint turned to me. "You may want to give the professor your film and have him drop it off for processing. I'll be anxious to see if that picture you took turns out. It looks like our next step will be to contact the Texas Rangers."

Clint spent the rest of the afternoon looking for clues as to what happened to the mysterious man who looked like John Morgan. When he had collected his thoughts, he called Ranger Estes.

"A body, you say? A male without any identification…Bring the dead man's wallet to me. I can have it tested by the morgue lab in Albuquerque for fingerprints and identification."

"Won't be easy if he's a foreign national," Clint said.

"I'm confident we can track down his history."

"The other man who got away was an officer."

"You mean he was a cop?"

"That's right. We're pretty sure he's the same guy who had something to do with Clayton's murder. Oh, and one other thing. We found a picture of Ariel in his pocket. In the photo, she was caught in the crosshairs of a gun. You might want to check that for fingerprints, too."

"Sure, will do." Ranger Estes said he would run the tests and put an all-points bulletin out on Morgan.

We learned later that Morgan had actually crossed the Arizona border and was in Silver City, New Mexico, heading into the Lower Mimbres on horseback.

"He couldn't have picked a better place to run to," Clint said. "My brother and I know the area like the backs of our hands. Our family also has a ranch there."

"You have relatives in New Mexico?"

"My brother, Julio. He's my spirit brother. We've known each other for a very long time. We're not descendants of the same family bloodline, but he is my Apache blood brother. Navajos and Apaches have similar ideas and beliefs. We met each other at the U.S. Naval Academy. He'll be able to help us track this sucker. I'll have him meet us at the line shack that we use during roundup."

That night it rained. Early the next morning, a large SUV with a horse trailer in tow was parked in the yard of the line shack with its headlights on.

"Get your butt up, Clint! I'm going to need some help with this stuff. I brought everything but the kitchen sink. Even some Indian ponies in case the traveling gets rough."

Julio had a quiet, husky voice, which held a note of urgency in it at the moment. Still blinking against the light, I thought that he was not at all as I'd pictured him in my imagination.

I hadn't thought he'd be so tall, or that his thick, dark hair would be shot through with bronze glints as it caught the light. Instead, I'd expected his features to be flatter and darker, more like the Mexican and Indian faces I had seen. But he had the straight nose of his Spanish ancestors, and a hard mouth that curved grimly when he became aware of my scrutiny.

"Well?" Julio asked in the same husky voice, and I got the sense that he was secretly laughing at my stunned, stupefied expression.

I found my tongue at last. "Do you really believe that you two aren't related?" For an instant, I had thought I was looking at the mirror image of Clint. "You could be twins," I said, extending my hand in welcome.

"A lot of people do say that." He laughed, the sun wrinkles creasing at the corners of his surprisingly hazel eyes. He warmly squeezed my hand in return. "And, you, my sister, remind me of a little yellow bird."

I would also be surprised later to learn that he lived in a two-story home and had a wife and two babies. Clint and his brother spent the next half hour or so unloading supplies while I prepared breakfast.

"Well, since we have that out of the way, suppose you tell me what's going on." Julio looked over at Clint as they each sat down to a plate of sausage and flapjacks.

"From what I could gather earlier, there are two sets of horse tracks that appear to be leading east toward Hidden Valley."

After Clint gave him a brief rundown of all that had transpired, Julio looked over at the two of us. "Are you ready to go?"

"I suppose," I said reluctantly.

"It would be a pleasure to introduce you to my father, Raoul, and his family."

CHAPTER X

After we left the line shack, it seemed like an endless journey to reach our destination. It was a place of awesome grandeur, a series of canyons and valleys that seemed to wind endlessly throughout the mountain range known as the Black Range.

I had not expected the valley to be so formidable; it took us four days to cross it. We traveled on foot, leading the horses more slowly than we had gone before since we were climbing upward. I felt myself ready to drop with weariness, although I knew better than to utter a murmur of protest. Clint had driven us hard, and even his own blood brother had grumbled at him that there was no need for such haste.

"What's the hurry, bro? We'll get there in the end."

When he spoke to me, Julio was extremely polite, always prefixing his requests with the word *Shi-da-zii*, which meant little sister.

Clint, on the other hand, paid me absolutely no attention unless he had to. I'd noticed he'd dropped his familiar terms of affection for me, and this had been replaced with a kind of distance. He would thank me when I handed him his food, warn me when the terrain ahead of us became rough or perilous, but that was all. It was as if the romance between us had never existed. I often found myself observing him, trying to figure him out.

Throughout our entire journey he had seemed preoccupied. He hardly spoke to either of us unless he was directly addressed, and he would sit by the fire when we made camp and stare away from the flame, into the distance. *What was he thinking of?*

Sitting by me one night, Julio followed the direction of my eyes and spoke softly. "My brother is a complicated person, eh? Even for me, he is not an easy person to know. But I can guess what he is thinking about. There is someone who holds a very special place in his heart, even though she is no longer alive. Because of his occupation, he feels she took a bullet that was meant for him. Finding that picture sheds a whole new light on things. I think he believes this guy Morgan may have had some involvement in her death."

"I'm sorry for Clint, I truly am, but he needs to get past this. That swine, Morgan, is not worth it. Is there anything we can do to help?"

"The best thing we can do right now is leave him alone. He needs to work it out for himself."

Was it my imagination, or did I hear sadness in Julio's voice? The next moment he shrugged, as if the matter was unimportant. "Perhaps it is better for your marriage, *Shi-da-zii*."

I didn't ask him what he meant by that. After a moment he stretched, yawning, and left me. I avoided the deep oozes of mud mixed with snow that still lay on the ground, all the while telling myself that I could not possibly walk another step.

What were we supposed to do now? Scale that precipitous cliff like mountain goats, and then think of a way to get around that jutting overhang that loomed menacingly?

Clint was looking up also when I returned, and I thought I saw some strange blend of emotion in his face. The obsession that I had sensed earlier in him was still there, but something else as well. Despair? Frustration? It was hard to tell. Perhaps something had gone wrong; perhaps he couldn't find the way to Hidden Valley with the snow still falling to the ground.

I watched him take a coiled length of rawhide from the saddle of one of the horses and put it around his neck. Then, without another word, he flattened himself against the sheer, rocky cliff face, and seemed to walk right off the edge. I think I must have gasped, for I saw Julio glance toward me.

"There is a path, *Shi-da-zii*. Not much, but the mountain goats made it long ago. That was how Clint found the way into the valley. Just wait and see. We will all find our way over there soon."

We waited for what seemed an endless time, but in actuality it was probably no longer than fifteen minutes. Eventually I saw a rope come snaking down. I realized that there must have been some kind of cleft up there between the huge, overhanging mountain edge and the rocky cliff I had dismissed as being unscalable. Now I stared at it in dismay.

Were we expected to crawl up that steep, rocky cliff face with nothing but a thin rope to support us? I turned to Julio, intending to make some protest, but he had already seized the dangling end of the rope. Using his feet for leverage against the sheer wall of rock, he began to clamber up it with surprising agility.

No sooner had he disappeared into what seemed like a tiny, shadowed cleft, than Clint came down, the rope sliding between his gloved hands. Without a word, he began to loop the end of the rope around one of the saddlebags Julio hauled up. I stood to one side, trying to hide the fact that I was getting angrier and angrier by the minute.

*I won't go up that ridiculous rope! If my hands were to slip...*I shuddered inwardly, trying not to think of it. Already my palms had begun to feel damp with sweat. Although I despised myself for cowardice, I had never cared for great heights. Why did I have to be faced with such a predicament? Continuing on this perilous mission was the height of folly! I never even liked flying on an airplane!

Clint must've sensed my fear, but did nothing to calm it. Even his next words seemed to carry an undertone of irony.

"It's your turn, Sarah. You're not afraid, are you?"

"Of course I'm not afraid!" I replied sharply. "But what are you going to do about the horses? How do you intend to get *them* up there?"

I think he knew I was procrastinating. The cleft in his cheek deepened, and he narrowed his eyes at me thoughtfully.

"You feel sorry for those two Indian ponies? You needn't be. They'll find food for themselves and be fine until my cousin Vinny and the others who are joining us shortly are ready to leave."

"You're not going to just leave them, are you?" I protested.

"They can look after themselves just fine. And if you don't get started, I'm going to have to tie one end of that rope around your waist and haul you up like one of those sacks!"

On that note, I took the rope in my hands. Looking back, I think it was only my anger that gave me the courage to scale that cliff face. I dared not look down. I was never more relieved than when I felt Julio's reassuring hands close around my wrists as he lifted me up onto a rock shelf that widened into a cave.

"Come, *Shi-da-zii*. We'll go this way."

With my knees still shaking, I followed him around a sharp bend. Then I saw a light at the other end of what was not actually a cave, but a tunnel-like fault in the mountain. *No wonder they called this Hidden Valley!* I could understand why it would be almost impossible to find, and how even one man with enough ammunition could hold off a whole army of attackers.

"My brother found this place when he came into the mountains alone to seek his medicine dream," Julio told me. "He saw a mountain goat that seemed to disappear, and he followed it. That was how he came upon the valley. See, *Shi-da-zii*? All around are the sides of the mountain, like walls. It is as if the mountains were split in the middle to make this place."

After we had emerged again into the daylight and began to scramble down the rocky slope into a meadow with gamma grass growing waist-high, I looked around in wonder. I thought I could see for miles ahead; the valley appeared narrow at this end, but I could see where it began to widen further on. The part I could see to my right was rocky and mountainous, with enormous boulders scattered about, as if they had rolled down the cliff many centuries ago when a gigantic earthquake or some other climatic event of nature had created this natural valley.

"It's beautiful!" I said.

Julio smiled with pride. "But you have seen so little yet. Wait until we travel further, and then you will see the true beauty. There is plenty of water here, and there are cattle and horses, too. They do well here, and the herds grow, but I can tell you it was a very difficult task to get them in here at the beginning."

"I suppose we have to walk again?" I said in a weary voice that was barely audible.

It was Clint who answered my question. "There are horses a few miles up ahead, in a small corral. Raoul always insists that they are kept here in case they are ever needed."

"How thoughtful," I murmured coldly. I saw Julio's eyes go back and forth between us, but he made no comment. He knew I was angry with my husband. Why should I pretend?

We walked forward again with Clint in the lead this time. Julio followed closely behind me. He seemed considerate, and it was his hand that closed around my arm when I stumbled. Clint didn't even turn his head to see if we followed or not.

I can't remember how far we walked. The valley widened and seemed to stretch before us like a miniature kingdom. The country to the left was flat and grassy for the most part; to the right, the terrain seemed rougher and split by deep, narrow gullies or arroyos, which Julio explained could become roaring watercourses in the summer, when the snow began to melt on the mountaintops.

The corral Clint had spoken of was a rough wooden enclosure. A half dozen restless, high-spirited animals of Arab stock pranced back and forth. Unlike modern-day Indians, this band of Apache didn't use saddles—only blankets thrown across a horse's back and bridles made of plaited horsehair. These hung in a small shed by the side of the corral ready for use, courtesy of Raoul and the men who tended his horses.

"Would you like to choose your horse?" Clint leaned his elbows on the rough fence beside me.

His gesture surprised me. I had always loved horses, and I couldn't pretend indifference.

"That one—the spotted mare. The breed is unfamiliar to me, although I believe I can detect some Arab blood in her."

"You're a pretty good judge of horseflesh, *hwe'esdzáán.*" Even the slightly sarcastic inflection of his voice when he called me the Navajo word for "one's wife" could not detract from the fact that he had actually paid me a compliment. "She's part Appaloosa, sired by the best show horse I ever saw, off an Arabian mare. You sure you can handle her?"

Was he challenging me again? I recalled the time that my brother and I took riding lessons. The instructor had allowed Clayton to ride unsupervised. Determined to keep up, I had convinced him that I was just as capable. The only problem was when we came to a three-foot jump: the horse had made the jump without me.

The high-spirited Arabian mare trotted nervously around the pen, tossing her head and snorting. She wasn't pleased about things at the moment. Standing in the middle of the round pen, I knew I was doing something wrong.

I realized she was anxious. "I'm trying to lower my energy level," I said as the mare ignored my physical cues to slow down, turn around, and come to me.

It didn't work. The animal turned toward me for an instant, then spun away, bucking. She wanted no part of this human. Slowly, almost imperceptibly, I changed my posture and motion. Only the mare noticed.

"I can feel her coming back to me," I said.

Now intently watching me, the horse stopped and slowly turned around as I directed her to do, then walked right up to me and put her head in my hands.

"Good job!" Clint cheered.

"May I ride her?"

"By all means," he nodded. "She's used to being guided by the pressure of your knees. Her name is Peyote. She's the best horse in the corral. You've chosen well."

In spite of my earlier foreboding, I could not help feeling a thrill of anticipation at being able to ride again. Clint was being almost affable for a change, and Julio seemed lighthearted away from his family responsibilities. After the horses had been saddled in the Apache fashion, we set out. It was Julio who complimented me next.

"I see that our Little Yellow Bird rides well," he commented to Clint, who merely nodded, his eyes looking over me without emotion. He looked like a man who had something eating at him on the inside, but why? I knew he'd held himself accountable for his wife's death. Is that what was still bothering him? I didn't think he was the kind of man who'd allow the memories of his deceased wife to destroy him.

"What's got into you?" I flung the words at him, but they sounded breathless and uncertain. He frowned, his lips twisting downward at the corners. I suddenly realized that I did not know him at all. He was the man

I planned my life around and hoped to live with for the rest of my life. How could we go on like this?

"Nothing's got into me," he answered calmly. "I would think that you'd be glad to see me have some time to myself. After all, it's not like you depend on me," he said in the same tone of voice.

He had been watching my face, and I suppose my expression gave me away. His cool manner annoyed me, and I think he knew that, too. "I'm sorry," he said suddenly, running his fingers through his long hair.

We skirted another deep, steep-sided canyon within the Black Range that seemed to climb to the mountain's edge.

Julio, riding close to me, spoke in a low voice. "My brother has a small cabin up there, a place he goes to when he wants to be alone. Even I have not been there. But then...I do not come here often. I prefer the comforts of my own people."

Every now and then I found myself forgetting that Julio was a White Mountain Apache tribal leader, and the father of two young children. Like his brother, he was something of an enigma. But it was Clint, in spite of everything I knew about him, who baffled me most.

Why did he want to be alone? I could better imagine him acting on sheer animal impulse. Was seeing his wife's picture the reason for his strange behavior? *If so, what was I doing here in the midst of all this intrigue, playing the part of a helpless pawn?* The thought struck me like a blow.

We were descending, almost imperceptibly, into a part of the valley that reminded me of a soup pot, with steam rising up from the hot springs. Even the climate seemed to have changed in some subtle way. There was no snow here, and the air seemed slightly warmer. The mountains that ringed us seemed to tower loftily and become even more impenetrable. Craggy peaks shrouded with snow hovered over us.

What am I doing here? How did I come to be here? I could not help feeling frightened by the challenge that lay ahead, and the eeriness of the land around me. It seemed like a little Apache haven, but how long had this valley lain here like a volcanic caldron waiting to erupt?

Julio had ridden ahead with Clint for the last few minutes, but now he dropped back, bringing his mount up beside mine. "You like what you have seen so far?"

"How could I not?" My response was honest. "It's uniquely beautiful. But…" I decided to speak aloud the question that had been puzzling me for some time. "Where are all the people? I've seen the cattle and horses; who looks after them?"

He smiled at me and then mustered a laugh.

"You have sharp eyes, *Shi-da-zii*. Yes, we have people who tend to the animals here—not many, but a few trusted men my father brought with him from the Fort Apache Reservation. No doubt they are at the house now, preparing their evening meal. It's getting late, and the sun drops from view early here. There's no need to watch for intruders in this place, for who could find it?"

"But surely your people know of this place?"

"A few do, but we respect the dwelling places of our friends and families. Sometimes, if a winter is very hard, we come here. There is always food and game to be found if we want it. My father Raoul and his brother Ramon, along with my cousin Vinny who came with us, they will all stay here for a while, until the hides we took are cured and the meat is smoked and packed away. And then they will return to the ranch."

I had the feeling that he might have said more if Clint had not swung his horse around and ridden back to us. As usual, I felt a tinge of resentment at his gaping look; it seemed to imply how untidy and unkempt I must look with strands of hair dangling down my face.

"It's not far from here now, but we'll stop for a while to rest the horses. If you want to take a bath or change clothes, there's a small stream back there behind those trees."

My hand went up to brush tendrils of hair from my face, and his mouth tilted at the corner.

"I'll give you ten minutes on your own, and then I'm comin' in, too. Need to wash off some of the trail dirt."

Under his sardonic gaze, I took the small pack containing my clean clothes from the back of the horse and walked without a backward glance in the direction he'd pointed.

Just as I reached the tiny mountain rill and was about to take off my clothes, I heard a husky voice. "Hurry up, little sister. I'm next!"

CHAPTER XI

My first impression when I saw Raoul walk down the steps of the rambling Spanish-style adobe and wood house was that he could not possibly be as old as he looked. Fading light still graced the sky, but the lamps had been lit and formed a background for the inlaid turquoise that sparkled in the elaborate Apache-style walking stick he held in his hand.

"My sons!"

His voice was rich and musical, and only slightly accented.

"*Si,* padre—your sons."

Raoul Navarro had crossed the Fort Apache land over the Arizona border into New Mexico three times, believing each time that he was a step closer to building a comfortable life for his wife and 14-month-old son in Hidden Valley.

The first two trips brought the 23-year-old ironworker to Silver City, New Mexico, where along with several other White Mountain Apache, he labored at mining and construction jobs, earning ten times more money than what he could scrape together on the reservation.

Navarro told his wife before setting off for the third time in 1948 that he would bring back fifteen hundred dollars in nine months—enough to finish building the rambling sprawling adobe lodge he referred to as "El Rancho."

But his luck ran out on his third trip. While he was away, tragedy struck and his wife passed away before they could move into their new abode. Raoul was a shaman, a tribal medicine man who used magic to cure the sick, divine the hidden, and control events.

He and Old Woman, who now looked after him, took great pains to see that Clint and I were comfortable. At the evening meal, they seated us together. It was such a beautiful place, and I found myself caught up in the people who lived there.

My eyes took in the whole family. I could feel the love shared by this clan. I noticed one young woman named "Little Dove." Her beauty was a younger reflection of her mother, Old Woman. The moment was spoiled when Clint announced he was going to visit Maria Venezuela, a medicine woman of the neighboring tribe, and also one of Clint's old flames.

The Old Woman called good-naturedly from the kitchen door. "Why are you going? Food not good enough for you?"

"It gets dark so early, and I've so far to go," my husband answered.

She walked past us without a word toward the stone mantle. She set her plate upon it, the contents of the little supper scarcely touched.

"I'll see you tomorrow," Clint called to her as she was walking away. She didn't respond.

Then he looked at me. "Sarah, you'll be fine here while I'm gone."

"Clint, why do you have to go visit someone you had a past relationship with? I feel like I should be jealous."

"There is no reason for you to be jealous. I'm not paying her a visit to rekindle a past fire. I need answers to questions—answers that only Maria can give. You have to trust me, Sarah. It's *you* that holds the key to my heart. I love you."

Having said that, he took me in his arms, kissed me, and told me he would be back by morning. It would be a long night for him on horseback.

Later on, I was surprised when the family adjourned outside to the fire pit. Old Woman, who had been in the shaman's lodge, came over and spoke in low tones to Little Dove. It turned out that the shaman had decided to make our relationship public. As the wife of his son's spirit brother, he felt some sense of paternal obligation toward me. Therefore it was decided that I should sleep in the lodge and consider it my home for as long as I remained in Hidden Valley.

Little Dove whispered to me that I was being shown a great honor; I noticed even her formidable-looking mother gave me a look of grudging respect. Then Little Dove told me I had to go with Old Woman. The old shaman, who was already lying wrapped in blankets before the coals, raised himself on his elbow and gave a nod of reassurance.

"It is the custom of our married guests to sleep in the lodge," he said in his dry, papery voice. "Sleep well, my children."

Old Woman motioned for me to follow her. I was unsure what to think of her. She continued to speak in several languages, a combination of English, Apache, and Spanish, as she led me through the large foyer. I started toward the door opening upon the steps with which I was already familiar, but here Little Dove's mother surprised and gratified me by suggesting that we take the servant's stairs.

We made our way through a room packed with supplies, such as rice and macaroni. It led into a large kitchen which looked as if it could've been an additional dining hall in medieval and early Renaissance days. There was a hearth in the far corner of the room. Pots, pans, and a grill served their purposes under the old, blackened turning-spit and pot hooks.

Little Dove's mother kept criticizing the impracticality of such an old kitchen, saying that it was too large and required too many steps. I shook my head, wondering why I felt that her friendly chatter was somehow at odds with her real nature.

Then she frowned slightly, pushing open a door that I assumed would lead to my bedroom.

I walked past her and turned around to bid her a good night, but she was gone. She had left her lantern on a table by the door. I looked around and noticed that my bed consisted of wool blankets and a small pillow. There was also a water pitcher and basin on another table.

At least in the morning, I'll be able to wash my face. I noticed a large ceramic receptacle underneath the table; so this was to be my bathroom, more commonly referred to as the chamber pot. As I undressed for bed, I worried about Clint finding me when he returned. I felt so alone in this room—almost like I had been abandoned. I told myself to stop dwelling on it. Clint would come back before morning and everything would be okay.

As I snuggled between the blankets, I realized that my whole life had changed so much within the space of a few days. I could hardly believe all this was really happening to me. As tired as I was, I should have gone right to sleep, but my mind was full of questions and I had no answers. When I finally did fall asleep, my dreams were frightening.

I was being chased across a high desert, and my feet kept sinking into the deep sand. I could hear the pulverizing footsteps of my pursuers close behind me. I knew both fear and despair when I found myself at the edge of a tall cliff, looking down into nothingness. Then I felt a hand clamp down on my shoulder, ready to push me over...

I woke up with sweat streaming down my face, but when I opened my eyes, it was only Old Woman that I saw. She had been trying to wake me. For a moment, the unreal appeared real. I was stiff in every limb, as if I'd actually been running, and I could still feel the blood pounding in my ears.

"Where is Clint?" I angrily asked.

She stared back at me uncomprehendingly, as though she didn't understand what I was saying. Then she put her hand over her mouth, shushing me. She quietly whispered. "The shaman is still asleep. He is an old man and likes to sleep late into the day."

I told her about my dream as I got dressed.

"Sometimes dreams portend certain events, and sometimes they hold warnings."

I wondered if my dream had been meant to warn *me* of the danger that I was facing.

The feeling of foreboding I had awakened with seemed to grow stronger as the day crawled by, so I tried to keep myself busy. I had already learned the women in an Apache camp were always kept occupied with one task or another. When they were not rounding up cattle or on hunting trips, the men sat in front of their modest dwellings, seeing to their weapons or making beaded jewelry.

Little Dove took me with her to gather roots and wild berries to prepare into a kind of paste for our journey. Her manner was much less reserved, and she talked to me as if we were truly friends. As we chatted, the subject of Maria came up. Little Dove mentioned that Maria was a powerful medicine woman who, at times, frightened her. In spite of my preoccupation, I noticed that on the few occasions she mentioned the journey that lay ahead, she would say things like "When you leave this valley…" or "When you leave the safety of this camp…"

"But you're coming, too, are you not?"

She gave me a startled, somewhat puzzled look. "I thought you had already been told. My stepfather is old and stubborn, and he wishes for me to stay here with him so that he can visit longer with my children, as they are like his grandchildren. Besides, he has forbidden me to enter the canyons."

Now it was my turn to look startled. "But why?"

"Anyone who ventures into the canyons risks the wrath of the *Chindi*, the dark, immortal forces of the underworld," she continued. "My mother told me this, and my aunt, who is a widow and looks after the shaman's brother, as well as the shaman, told me what he said. Apparently they heard the shaman and your husband speak of this long before you ever came to this land. If I had known you were to travel with Clint, our spirit brother to the canyons, I would have warned you before your arrival to this camp. I don't suggest you go there. If you do, make sure you stay alert."

I looked into her concerned face and swallowed what I had almost said. She wouldn't have understood my anger. I would save the scathing speeches I had stored up all day for Clint, the next time I confronted him.

As it turned out, I did not see him at all that day. The women found tasks to keep me busy and I followed their laughing directions. Inside I seethed with anger, furious at Clint's long absence to visit his old flame.

That evening, the old shaman ceremoniously presented me with the traditional Apache costume. "Our women would rather wear the garments of the white women now than the buckskin garments that their mothers took such pride in wearing," he said in his dry voice.

"These belonged to Rowena, who was the mother of my son Julio. She wore them when I took her as my wife before the whole tribe. It would please an old man's heart if you would accept them, my daughter."

The traditional Apache woman's costume consisted of a long skirt reaching just above the ankles, richly embroidered with beads and quills. The high-necked over-blouse was just as heavily embroidered, carefully fringed at the yoke and sleeves as the skirt had been.

"It would also please me if you wore these garments when you continue on your journey. Perhaps they will protect you from harm and bring you good luck."

"I'm proud that you would give these to me," I murmured. I could not help wondering if this old man with his seamed and wrinkled face had loved his young bride. Had she loved him in return?

These old stories constantly reminded me of a past I'd had no part of. How was I supposed to react to all this? Even my husband was becoming more and more of a stranger to me. What did he expect of me?

The shaman, my spirit father, seemed to take his duties seriously. There were other gifts: moccasins, a suede tunic and matching leggings, and a bear necklace for protection. It was the thought itself and the blessings bestowed that pleased me most of all. I tried to thank him, but his face became closed.

"I had a dream last night. All this was meant. Your husband, who should have been a shaman of his own people, saw it first."

But what could he have seen, I wondered, *when he didn't even know if I would agree to come here?*

"You are in grave danger, my daughter. Your destiny is being fulfilled, and your husband is powerless to help you." Again the shaman seemed to have the power of reading my thoughts. "You are still unsure about Clint, are you not?"

"How can I help it? He has been so insensitive and distant. When he left last night, he told me to trust him. How can I? He's been gone now for almost twenty-four hours!"

"He has his reasons for visiting Maria. It has nothing to do with her. It has everything to do with you."

"I know that you, my father, have always believed in him, but what of the way he's been acting? Ignoring me, running off to that woman, and then not returning to the camp! Doesn't he realize that it's unacceptable behavior?"

"Why don't you ask him?" The old man's voice was as soft as the rustling of dry leaves.

"Ask him?" I realized that my voice had risen, so I tried to control it. "He would only ignore me, as he has done before. Or grow angry with me."

"You, my daughter, are trying to vilify his visit with Maria. You think it's something more than just asking questions. You must give Clint a chance to explain his actions."

This old man might have been my own father, or my grandfather, who had first taught me about logic and justice. My eyes dropped under his calm, steady gaze. "You really think I should ask him?"

"It is what *you* think, my daughter. And what you must ask yourself. I can only tell you that Clint is headstrong, and he is angry. But if you can put aside your resentment and ask him what worries you and what worries him, he will answer you. I have spoken to him, and he will show you the respect that is due a wife. That is all."

He sighed. "Peace can be achieved only if people will sit down together and speak of those things that trouble their minds. It is easy to be angry. It is more difficult to say, 'I will find out what is troubling my husband, and I will try to understand.'"

"You make it sound so easy."

There was no one in the world I would rather be with than Clint, but I couldn't help wonder how this would all end.

The old man looked at me through sleepy eyes. "We will speak again before you depart for the canyons."

First thing the next morning, Old Woman offered to fill the tub for a bath for me, which was a blessing. Afterward, remembering my promise to the shaman, I put on the traditional Apache suede tunic, leggings, and moccasins he had given me and combed my damp hair so that it hung loosely at my shoulders.

"Rather chic!" I complimented myself. Old Woman looked at me and nodded her approval.

I followed her into the kitchen, where she handed me a piece of fry bread. As I nibbled on it I gazed out the window, wondering where the hell Clint was. He must know that I would be worried since he hadn't come back when he said he would. He couldn't *still* be visiting Maria. All my resentment was simmering just under the surface.

I saw Julio loading supplies on the horses—but there was only two of them. Surely Clint would be back soon, knowing we were leaving for the canyons today.

I walked out to the yard. "Where are the other horses?"

"More horses will only slow us down, little sister. Look at you—you are an Apache now—walking will come easily to you, I'm sure."

"You're not serious, are you, Julio? It's a long journey."

I heard footsteps behind me. Clint was walking toward us, but he didn't say a word to me. I felt as if everyone was watching me, and I felt judged. The two women who were to accompany us were waiting good-naturedly in spite of the heavy packs they carried on their backs. Clint stood beside his brother; his face, as usual, was unreadable.

Isn't this just great, I thought to myself. *He's been gone more than two days, and he doesn't say a word to me.* I could not lose control of my anger, so I shrugged lightly instead, hating myself for the gesture. "Of course, I should've guessed, shouldn't I? We're walking."

"When you see the kind of country we have to travel over, I think you'll understand," Clint said quietly.

The shaman, who had made it a point to arise early today, stood to face us, his mouth curved up in a smile. "Take comfort in the Blessing of the Apaches. May you have a safe journey."

As we set out, Julio scouted the ground for tracks. "Looks like our dude is headed into Devil's Canyon."

"Nobody would be that foolish, not even Morgan," Clint said, staring down at the pointed boot marks.

"It's a straight-shootin' path; a toe mark, a boot depression, and a smoothing out of every track with several brush strokes across the dirt."

Julio stood ramrod-straight in his crisp, clean jeans and Wrangler snap-button cowboy shirt. He admitted being a bit defensive about his reputation as a tracker. "I'm telling you, that's where he's headed."

"Apaches really can be a hard-headed bunch," Clint grumbled, taking up his reins and beginning to lead his horse.

I guessed this meant we were taking a detour through Devil's Canyon. I had not expected it to be so formidable that it would take us two hours to reach the first tier of caves. The incline halfway up the snowy slope was steeper than anything I'd previously stood on. Clint figured it was thirty-five degrees; Julio guessed fifty. It was probably half that. One misstep would have sent us sliding down the slope to our death.

Midday, at 10,800 feet, we reached the ridge that ran between Devil's Canyon and its neighbor, Mount Negro, New Mexico's most challenging peak. We walked toward a cavernous opening in a depression on the ridge. It was empty, so we hunched behind some nearby rocks to get out of the wind. I gnawed on a cracker spread with the paste that Little Dove had prepared for us.

Continuing our quest, we trudged on in the thin air, up a gently sloping ridge with a large, overhanging cornice that led to the first of three false summits. The wind, twenty mph or more, shoved us toward the edge and an enormous snowy bowl far below. The billowy clouds that raced overhead cast huge, eerie shadows on the snow. They provided little comfort to me as I moved along an exposed ridge, thinking about all the horror stories I had heard about Devil's Canyon.

"People say that this is the dwelling place of the evil spirits."

"It wouldn't surprise me," I said to Julio, looking back down at the abyss that seemed to be bubbling up like a giant caldron of exhaust fumes. It seemed like the perfect home for the *Chindi*.

"Did you know about this?" I looked over at Clint. "Is this your idea of a sick joke?"

He didn't answer at first.

"I know that a crazy old medicine man who dresses up in a bovine costume and goes by the name Yellowhair resides in one of the caves, but he's harmless."

Perhaps Clint figured we could still catch up with Morgan. After all, we'd done our share of hiking. I'd descended the Grand Canyon, Clint had climbed Mount McKinley in Alaska, and Julio had hiked the Ña Pali cliffs of Hawaii.

In retrospect, our naiveté was comical. Ten days earlier on our drive in, approaching the Lower Mimbres, we'd debated whether Mount Negro would have snow on the slopes. As we'd crested a rise in the highway and the mountain rose before us, we'd seen a blanket of its first snow glistening in the sun.

Even after we knew the brilliant white slopes had fresh snow, we still hadn't brought snowshoes or crampons, assuming the snow would soon melt seeing how it was the middle of August. We had one pole between us. Clint was leading, poking the snow with it. To add to my woes, the moccasins the shaman had given me rubbed my heels raw. I tried walking backward, which did ease the pain, but my progress was pitifully slow because I had to look over my shoulder. I knew that if I ambled off a ledge I'd feel incredibly foolish. The two women were leading the supply horses.

At the second tier of ledges, Morgan's tracks disappeared. Unbeknownst to us, Morgan was secretly keeping track of *us*. By this time the wind was blowing thirty mph. From our vantage point, we studied the faint line of the river, the white buttes and red rocks, the rolling hills dotted with green bristlecone pines and the small enclave of Hidden Valley.

I'd like to say that I spent my time in deep appreciation of our majestic surroundings, but in reality, I was hurting, cranky, and preoccupied with returning to Cornflower Corners as soon as possible. To hell with Morgan, and to hell with my inept tracking companions. I was more than ready to turn back.

The steep walk up the mountain had also hurt my lungs; going back down in the mucky, melting snow damaged my blistered heels. By the time we returned to the line shack, I was dehydrated, famished, and nauseated from the high altitude. I changed into some dry clothes and comfortable shoes. Our vehicles were a sight to behold. Clint and Julio chatted about us leaving, and sending the women back to Hidden Valley with the supply horses.

I examined my ravaged feet while a group of adventurous teens who had arrived in an old truck partied in the yard of the line shack. Given my pounding headache, their carefree laughter was galling.

We should have spent the night at the line shack, but we were anxious to get home. The thought of sharing the site with the noisy teens was not inviting. By midnight, Julio, Clint, and I reached the Arizona-New Mexico line. Dawn was not far away when I finally saw the well-lighted, horse-headed columns of the ranch.

As for Morgan, he had eluded us...*again*.

CHAPTER XII

During the weeks that followed, the reality of Morgan's inexplicable escape ate at Clint. He became like a man obsessed. Julio confided that he felt he had to tiptoe around his brother, and I avoided him as much as possible. I found myself spending more and more time alone since Clint spent all *his* time traveling with his ongoing investigation. We never discussed his visit with Maria.

On one of the rare occasions he remained at Cornflower Corners, Clint slid silently into his chair, folding his body over the table like a bent cigarette. He looked haggard with the black circles under his eyes and his sunken cheeks.

A new housekeeper in a brocade vest and gloves took our breakfast order.

"Gloves at ten thirty in the morning?" Clint looked over at the Frenchman with the spiked hairdo. I gathered from his expression that he was having a difficult time adjusting to the male housekeeper I had hired. Pierre was the same waiter who had received his walking papers from the Scottsdale Fireside Inn.

"Just coffee for me," Clint said sourly. "Black."

I asked for a large orange juice, a bowl of shredded wheat flavored with apples and almonds, and *mille-feuille*, a French pastry that Pierre made from scratch every day. Let Clint suffer. *I* was hungry.

"That was some squeeze that bear put on that fellow in the cave," he began reflectively. "I've never seen a corpse look so bad, with brains dangling out of his head."

"Your breakfast conversation is most appetizing."

"Just thought you should know," he said. "I've been at the morgue most of the night with Ranger Estes. He kept the body in the cooler until I could get back so that both of us would be able to go over the remains."

"The way you look, you're lucky they let you out."

He ignored me. "They got a fingerprint from the dead man that matched a partial print taken back in 1992 on the reservation where your brother was killed. And guess what?"

I didn't have to guess. I had figured all along that Morgan was involved. I just didn't know if he'd had accomplices. Now I pictured him dashing around, frantically trying to cover his tracks, hopefully freaking out with his fifth accomplice dead.

"Incidentally, I picked up that picture you took of the looters, but it turned out too grainy to be recognizable." Clint sagged back in his chair and turned toward the sprawling hibiscus that threatened to overrun the porch. Everything was quiet for a while. Then he turned to me. "I'm leaving again for Albuquerque tonight. I just came home to pack a few things."

Why did he feel the need to go to Albuquerque again, I wondered? Seeing how I wasn't getting anything except mosquito-bitten and angry, I went back into the house.

I was dozing when the telephone rang. I picked it up on the first ring, just to stop the noise. At this time of night, it was usually a boiler room call, somebody selling time-shares in Arizona or beachfront condos in Mexico. I wasn't expecting it to be the police.

"This is Sergeant José Hernandez in Valencia County, New Mexico. I just received a message from your husband, Clint."

"Is he all right?"

"Yes. He says he wants you to meet him at his cabin in New Mexico."

"Do you know what he wants?"

"He didn't say. Just told me his cell phone wasn't working. He said he'll expect you in four days."

Since I wasn't traveling the distance from the line shack, it should really only take me three days. If I started out on the south pasture entrance, I could shave off another day, even though I'd be on foot.

"Where is that new housekeeper?" I grumbled, beginning to pack up my things.

Magically, Pierre appeared. "What are you doing packing at this time of night?"

He stood watching me load up on water and beef jerky.

"Clint asked me to meet him at the cabin in New Mexico."

"You can't leave at this hour of night," he protested, following me around the kitchen.

"I have to; that way I can get a fresh start in order to make the climb to Hidden Valley."

"Please, *mademoiselle*," he implored me as I walked out the door. "You mustn't…"

CHAPTER XIII

As I drove, my mind was going a hundred miles an hour. I needed a horse to get to the bottom of the cliff. Clint had told me about a ranch just inside of New Mexico, so I would stop there. I could borrow a horse and trailer, and I could make it in a day and a half, instead of two.

I made good time getting to New Mexico. I was lucky that the people at the ranch were early risers. I met with Andy, the ranch foreman, explained who I was, and that I needed to get to Clint. He had no problem loaning me a gentle mare and a trailer. He even offered to send someone with me to bring her back.

I told him he could just send someone in a few days to pick her up at the fire tower. He loaded her into the trailer, fully saddled with a loose girth. I hooked up to the trailer and headed for the south pasture entrance.

The slopes of the Black Range became more thickly forested, the scent of piñon and alder sweet in the clear, cool air. The mountains seemed pristine, untouched; there were none of the ugly scars left by miners seeking precious metals. It seemed as if nothing had ever dwelled here but the wild creatures who called this their natural habitat. I did not have to be told this was Indian country.

I unloaded the mare and tightened the cinch. Black thunderheads were forming overhead, mountainous clouds picking up the moisture from the nearly fifty-yard-wide river. It was nearly noon and the world was gray. It was seven miles up a steep narrow canyon to the Black Range.

I checked my gear—the beef jerky, the water, a disposable camera—all safely tucked away in a thin pouch. I mounted the mare, took a deep breath, and headed into the deep ravine hunched over the body of this gentle mare. "God be with us," I whispered to her.

Blackish-brown beavers slid into the water from the side of the trail, their broad flat tails flapping as they landed. Some were babies, two feet in length, looking like ceramic replicas from a hotel gift shop. The adults, three or four feet, launched themselves into the water with strong webbed hind feet. Some piled brush along the bank, forming dams to trap the water and keep cool.

I took the camera from out of my pouch. The playful creatures frolicked in the river water for quite a while before noticing they were being photographed. I stopped the horse to see if I could get a close-up shot. I didn't have long to wait. They bobbed their heads in and out of the water and snarled at me, showing off two big yellow incisors. Then, without so much as a glance in my direction, they quietly swam away. I stuffed the camera back in my pouch.

I rode parallel to the river until I came to the part where the woods were the densest. I reined the horse in a thicket that partially concealed it and offered it a patch of grass to graze. Then I looked back in both directions. I kept feeling like I was being watched. Seeing nothing, I started the slow, hazardous climb up the mountain.

The dark clouds were getting closer and the wind was kicking hard from the west as I rode south into the canyon, my knees practically up to my chin. Some serious wild desert bighorn sheep were hurrying back on the path, their sure-footed hooves crunching over the ground, heads down. One white-bearded ewe with knobby knees was apparently having a hard time with her descent, taking not one step, but two.

The lightning crackled as I continued on my way. I drove my horse up the narrow, steep-sided canyon that seemed to cut its way up into the highest mountain peak.

I rode for miles, taking in the beauty of the land. The mare was a comfortable ride. It was almost dusk when I arrived at the fire tower, a charming wooden structure with a long, elevated ramp leading to a circular deck fifteen feet above the saw grass.

It was deserted except for the animals. Birds fed along the banks of a pond below, keeping a watch for the rattlers that lurked nearby. I released the mare under a mountain ash in the fenced area around the fire tower. Then I grabbed my gear and slowly walked up the ramp, listening for human sounds. Birds in the trees chirped, and little splashes came from the pond below, but I heard nothing more. I decided that the tower would be a great place to rest for a few hours; from here the journey would be all on foot.

Inside the top of the fire tower, I caught the glint of the sun, hidden by the clouds, preparing to drop off into the horizon. A large hawk flew by, carrying a small rodent. A small unseen animal rustled the saw grass below. I took a piece of beef jerky out of my pouch and gnawed on it. Then I made myself a bed on the couch. I was fast asleep as soon as my head hit the cushion.

I awoke way before dawn, feeling an urgency to be on my way. I made sure the mare was secure in her area and headed out. I could not shake the feeling that I was being watched by someone.

I made my way up the face of the cliff; it was more circuitously than if I were traveling with Clint and his brother. I didn't take the same steep path used by Julio and those who carried burdens. I scrambled upward instead, foot by foot toward the second tiers of stone and the first broad ledges.

Some forty feet from the ground on a broad ledge, I looked out across the valley. The sky was very gray with black clouds. The last leafage, seared crusty brown, was on the trees and bushes. Only one other visitor besides Clint and me had come to Hidden Valley this summer.

A trader from a neighboring village had brought medicinal plants and had traded skins in exchange for amethyst from the mine. He had stayed for ten days. Clint and I had arrived four days later. I had been hoping he would still be here.

I recalled how the shaman had scratched out the sign of the Hidden Valley people at the mine load and drawn the sign of the bear over it instead. I wore that same sign on my necklace among the beads, the claws, and the threaded shells. I was looking forward to seeing Raoul and his family.

Suddenly I heard voices from somewhere behind me. They seemed far away, but I crouched very still, hoping that whoever they were, they would choose another path. But the noises came closer. Then I saw the dim glow of flashlights. *Were they after me? Who were they?*

My breath caught in my throat as I watched them move ever closer. I saw three figures moving swiftly, crouched over, carrying baseball bats. They emerged from the brush into the clearing. Now I began to panic. *What could they possible want from me?*

I seemed frozen in place as they drew near enough for me to see that they wore headbands. Then I saw the others. My foot dislodged a small pebble and I heard it drop away from me to the left. It made a clear sound as it struck the stone below.

I struggled to my feet. Gasping, I reached for the stone sides of the mountain. Frantically I began to scramble up the cliff, my fingernails breaking in the rough crevices. From the ledge below me, the flashlights were brighter. I crouched on the ledge and tried to figure out what to do.

I climbed another foot, then I heard a man's voice cry out to me to return to the ledge. Desperately I sought a new handhold. He yelled at me again. I finally found a handhold and moved higher on the cliff. A rock struck me hard on the left side, right above the small of my back. I slipped, but managed to catch myself.

Then I heard the man begin to follow me. I could hear another male with him. I reached a small ledge. Breathing wildly, I grasped a heavy stone with both hands. Then I raised it over my head and flung it downward. It struck the first climber a glancing blow on the side of his head. He lost his hold, scrambling and scratching against the side of the cliff. Then he skidded and dropped, falling back to the broad ledge, twenty feet below.

The second climber reached over the ledge on which I stood and grabbed my ankle. I shook his hand free and scrambled upward. He leaped for me, but I was too high for him. I found the rope and shinnied up it, pulling it up behind me.

The man did not climb up after me, but stood on the ledge shouting at me instead. Twice he threw rocks. One struck me on the left leg, behind the knee. The other struck near my face on the left side, nearly causing me too lose my hold, but again I did not fall. I heard more men shouting below. I sensed that they were looking for a new, easier ascent to head me off. My fury temporarily overcame my fear. I began picking up rocks and hurling them down at my pursuers.

The man below me was now making his way upward. He shouted angrily at me as he dodged my rocks. He gestured over and over that I should come down. I threw one more rock and felt great satisfaction when he swore painfully. Then I climbed some more. I slipped and cried out, but that didn't stop me.

I hung to the cliff a yard below its summit, but I couldn't reach it. I was more than eighty feet above the nearest outjutting ledge below me at this point, the height of an eight-story building. I didn't dare turn and look back toward the valley, which lay some two hundred feet below. Instead I wept, and put my cheek against the granite of the cliff. Never before had I tried to scale the cliff on this face. With a sick feeling in my stomach, I realized that I hadn't chosen the right ascent.

I had seen Julio climb the cliff at this point, but he was powerful and long of limb. The original path, I now remembered, had been to my left. I could not retrace my steps now without falling into the hands of my pursuer. He laughed below me, sensing my predicament. I cried out in misery. Suddenly I felt the wind moving against me on the cliff; I was terrified of falling.

I heard a sound above me—a clicking noise, a whinny, and snort. Peyote looked over the cliff, pawing at the ground. What was she doing out of her corral? Then I saw my opportunity. I reached for the rope with my one free hand, swung it out over the cliff, and snagged the horse's head in the noose.

"Back Peyote, back!" I shouted.

The man below cried out with rage, but inch by inch, Peyote, with her squat, powerful body, drew me to the summit of the cliff. I gratefully scrambled over it. I collapsed in the thick layer of dust and seeds from the low brush and the twisted, stunted trees. I heard a cry behind me; the man pursuing me had gained the height of the cliff.

Suddenly I saw two men appear some two hundred yards away, emerging over the rocks. I moaned. *Two more pursuers coming from another direction!* My mind in a quandary, I turned back, and then back again. They were approaching swiftly. I didn't know which way to run.

Then I felt the hand of the man behind me in my hair. He painfully threw me to my knees on the stone. I tried to reach his hand in my hair. Peyote tossed her head back, causing the rope to snap, and then darted away. The other men were getting closer, so I tried to struggle. My captor wrenched my head viciously back and forth. I saw Peyote stop, and look about wildly. I lifted my hand to the horse, tears in my eyes. The two other men were now within fifty yards.

To the astonishment of the man who held me, Peyote suddenly turned back and reared up, her hooves landing on his back. As he was struggling with the horse, his right arm let go of me, and I scrambled away. Grabbing the rope that hung from Peyote's neck, I hoisted myself up on her. I heard the other two men behind me, and the cry of yet another man from somewhere else. I kicked Peyote and we fled.

I thought I saw a dim orange glow high above me, but the lightning was too close and too fierce for me to judge properly. The thunder echoed against the narrow rocky walls; it seemed to surround me and split my eardrums open.

"Clint!"

I screamed his name frantically and uselessly between cannon-like explosions of sound. I thought I heard the noise of rushing water. My mare, as frantic and frightened as I had become, stumbled and then scrambled for balance as she headed for the least steep portion of the rock-encrusted walls.

I had lost the rope that dangled from Peyote's neck and clung tenaciously to her mane. The ominous onslaught of the rain seemed to beat angrily against my face and body. I had never known such rain before. It was almost a solid sheet of water that attacked me viciously.

Peyote stumbled, almost throwing me, and then her hooves found a foothold and she started up a seemingly unscalable cliff. In a sudden flare of whitish light, I saw the water that swirled as high as my ankles. I frantically lifted my legs up to the mare's withers as a wall of water roared down the wash toward us.

"Clint!"

Lightning flooded everything with a blinding flow of white fire, and I screamed once more before the thunder came on its heel, making me cower. Crouching down, I guided Peyote, taking shelter against the cliff. I heard the high, bleating scream of a sheep from somewhere below me and did not dare look down, although my senses told me what had happened.

It was most likely the white-bearded ewe that had been swept away by the water. Soon, when my hands were too cold and too numb to keep holding on, I too would be carried down the wash like a piece of debris. A floating log smashed against my thigh and I screamed again in despair, my hands still clinging to my mare with all the strength that was left in me.

And just when I had lost all hope, I imagined I heard Clint's voice from somewhere above me. I screamed his name again with all the force and breath left in my lungs.

"Clint! Oh Clint, hurry please!"

The rain had let up a bit. Then I heard his voice again; this time it was clear. I almost didn't believe my own ears; it just didn't seem possible.

"Sarah? Jesus Christ! Hang on, do you hear? Wait!"

I began to sob helplessly, the breath rasping in my throat. I clung to my mare's mane, only too conscious of the water that was swirling around us.

A rope snaked down from above me somewhere and hit me square in the face.

"Sarah! Can you hear me? Catch the rope! Can you hold onto it?"

"I…I think I can!" I sobbed out the words.

"Try to get it around Peyote's neck. It's a slipknot, a hangman's noose. If you can loop it around, you should be able to guide her up."

The rope dangled in front of my face, slapping wetly against my cheeks with every gust of wind. I forced myself to loosen the fingers of my right hand, deliberately trying to close my mind to the sucking sound of the water below me. With one hand, I fumbled with the knot, pulling the loop wide.

I heard Clint's voice above me, and wondered why it sounded so shaken and rough.

"Sarah! For God's sake, try to hurry! You can do it, just don't look down. Get the rope around Peyote's neck…now tug on it when you're ready."

My mind gave me commands and I obeyed them by instinct. I forced the loop over Peyote's head, but it was no great feat compared to the time I had roped her from the side of a cliff. I felt my body slide backward on her. As I tugged on the rope, her body moved forward.

My suede jacket smashed against the side of the canyon wall and ripped. What did it matter? At least we were being led higher and higher. I heard the water let go of us with an angry, sucking sound. It was just below us now. Finally we made it to the top safely. The storm had turned into a drizzle.

"Sarah! Dear God, what are you doing out here in this storm?"

"Didn't you send for me?"

"Hell no!" He looked puzzled. "Did you think I'd make you take this type of trip alone?" His voice sounded harsh, yet his hands were gentle enough as they pushed the hair off my face.

"Oh, Sarah," he said softly. "You mean so much to me. I just don't want to disappoint you."

"The only way you could ever disappoint me is if you stopped loving me."

"I could never do that. Can you make it to the cabin?" he asked. "It's only a few minutes away. You can probably see the firelight from here. We'll talk when we get there," he promised as he mounted his horse.

I turned Peyote toward the firelight in the distance. "Yes, I'm sure I can make it that far. We should hurry, though. I had three or more men following me up the cliff."

I felt cold and wet as our horses carried us toward the cabin, but being with Clint made me feel safer.

"Let's get you out of the rain and into some dry clothes," he said as we approached the cabin. Its front door was partially propped open, and a welcome fire was snapping and crackling inside.

I clung to his outstretched hand as I climbed off my horse, gasping as we walked up the ramp. I stood on the deck of the alpine structure, hunched over the rail, looking down at the pond below.

Then I saw a man emerge from the clearing and walk hurriedly up the path. It was Julio.

"Damn, woman! You put a scare into me," he said as he ran the rest of the way up the ramp. "I got a strange call from Pierre. He said you were on your way up here to meet Clint. I decided to come and make sure that everything was okay."

"Everything's fine, bro," Clint answered as he stood in the open doorway. "I'm glad you came, though. I've been concerned about Sarah myself." He looked at me with his tawny-green eyes. "Take this gun and keep it with you at all times." Then he looked back at Julio. "I'm worried that something may happen to Sarah because of my dream…"

"What dream?"

"It was the same one that my father had," Julio answered. "The dreams of a shaman are never without some deeper significance. Perhaps it will be Clint who saves your life someday. He dreamed of a yellow bird pursued by hawks, all flying blindly into a coyote's den. Two of the hawks soared upward looking for other prey, but the other dropped down like an arrow from the sky and slashed at the yellow bird with his sharp beak and talons. Suddenly two eagles drove the hawk away and the yellow bird was free again. It flew away under the shadow of the eagles' wings."

I frowned at him. "What a horrible dream! And if I were a bird, I'm sure I'd be a hawk instead of some silly frightened canary."

He shook his head and moved casually to a window that was always cracked open; it let breezes of clear air in for breathing.

"Clint says he enjoys the cabin and the peace it offers. It's the perfect place for meditation and retreat. A bird sings, a crow caws, and you can hear the scurrying of a ground squirrel in the underbrush. For me, it's complete solace. I go there to relax. I look at the stars and the moon at night. It renews me."

I was unaware that I had torn my pants and scraped skin off my knee. I had just sat down at the kitchen table with Clint and Julio for a beer when I heard a howling sound come from one of the guest rooms upstairs.

The noise came again, a little louder this time. Julio heard it and turned toward Clint, his eyes wide. Then they both bounced up over the stairwell railing and charged up the staircase. A few minutes later they came back.

"Nothing to be concerned with," Clint assured me. "Just the wind whistling through a window that was left open a crack."

I wasn't convinced, especially when Clint admitted he had sensed something.

He crossed to the refrigerator and then abruptly stopped. He stood there with his hand on the door, staring out the kitchen window that faced the woods. I could tell that Julio also sensed something; his intuition was always on target.

"One first feels the presence of the *Chindi* through its black aura," he said in an ominous tone. "It's definitely a dark presence."

"Not the *Chindi* again."

Clint was still staring out the window with one hand curled around the handle of the refrigerator. I began to feel frightened. There seemed to be something in the air, something almost between urine and musk—it wafted in through the open window and made the hairs on my arms rise. The back of my neck also began to tingle.

Then Clint opened the fridge door and the mood shifted. "How about another beer, bro? It's good and cold."

"Sure."

"How about you, Sarah?"

"Yes, please. I could use one with all I've been through."

Clint walked over to the kitchen table and handed us each a beer. Then he sat down and joined us. "Tell my brother and me what happened, Sarah."

"First of all, how did you know I was in danger? How did you come to my rescue?"

"I'd just gone out to gather firewood before the storm hit, and I felt my name being called through the wind," Clint answered. "I knew it was you. Now tell us what happened."

"As best I can remember, it happened something like this. From the moment I left the fire tower, several men wearing headbands and carrying baseball bats were after me. I counted three, then six. They came to corner me on a ledge. That's when Peyote came to my rescue. She saved my life," I said simply at the end of my harrowing saga.

Clint put his hand on my shoulder. "Do you believe these men are still after you?"

All the bizarre things that had happened roiled around in my mind. Hell, it all seemed insane. *Or was I?*

"No," I said at last. "I still don't understand what happened. They must have been after me for some reason—the goons with the baseball bats, I mean—because they chased me for a long time."

I thought of the yellow bird pursued by hawks in the dream. One of the hawks had attacked the yellow bird while the others flew away. "The goons on the ledge are the hawks. Peyote is symbolic of the mythical eagles that rescued the little bird, right?"

Clint didn't answer.

"How about another beer, bro?" Julio asked him.

"No, thanks. I've got to get some more firewood," Clint said reluctantly.

"I may as well go, too."

Julio started to walk away, then turned back. "Man, you know what? I caught a glimpse of a couple of weird-looking guys when I came into the line shack campsite."

"What was so weird about them?"

Julio shook his head. "I don't know, but they were wearing headbands and carrying baseball bats. I suppose they could have been hunting rabbits."

"Whoever heard of hunting rabbits with baseball bats?"

"It's a modern adaptation," Clint explained. "In the old days, they hung a net or constructed a tight fence across a narrow place. Some men waited there with sticks while others walked through the brush to drive the rabbits toward the trap. It used to be a community tradition; now it's become a pastime among the younger generation."

"Just be careful," Julio warned me as he went out.

"And keep the doors locked," Clint added, waving as he headed off.

I began to feel chilly as I walked into the living room, so I picked up the afghan that was on the sofa and put it around my shoulders. There were only a few embers left in the fireplace. Suddenly I was overcome by all my emotions as I stood in front of the window in the dim firelight. I realized I had been riveted to the same spot by the curtains since Clint had left to get firewood.

A low, guttural sound—close to a grunt throbbed from just outside the door. I barely had time to realize that it couldn't have come from Clint. Then the door flew open with a thud. Ducking reflexively, I narrowly avoided the hand reaching in to seize me. Whoever had called me on the phone to lure me to the cabin must've been hiding outside the door. Concealed by the gloom, he had waited until Clint and Julio departed to make his move.

I heard deep panting and felt his hot breath as he made another lunge at me. Again I managed to evade his grasp, shying away from him like a spooked colt. Having no time to think clearly, I had unknowingly given my assailant the advantage, placing him between the door and myself. Before I could turn and try to make my escape, the door violently slammed shut.

The dark figure flew at me. A hand closed around my wrist and I was thrown back against wall of the living room. Surprised and alarmed, I saw the dark figure come closer. Its face was partially hidden by the cowl-like jacket. Before I could run, thick legs were blocking me. Huge bulging arms and thighs were moving toward me.

I had managed somehow to escape the earlier ambush, but not this one. I was truly trapped this time.

The man moved into the softly glowing patch of firelight and grinned. Only then did I recognize my captor. Horrified shock all but robbed me of speech. "Morgan! But how…? What…?"

"My, aren't you surprised to see me again." John Morgan's badly scarred face was distorted into a cynical grimace. His hate-filled eyes glowed red in the reflected light. A black hooded jacket was wrinkled and wet on his stout form. In the scuffle, the hood had fallen around his shoulders; it revealed patches of coarse, matted hair that lay about his head like the ridgeback mane of a wild beast. He crouched as though he intended to leap the short distance between us, but then I remembered that this was his usual way of standing.

"I'm certainly pleased to see you, my dear," he continued in a sardonic voice. "That's why I broke out of jail and tracked you here to have a reunion."

"What do you mean?" I gasped. "What exactly are you saying?"

"I'm saying that you're going to have to pay this time."

I felt the blood begin to drain from my face. "Morgan, what is it that you want? Answer me!"

"I'll give you an answer, you bitch!" Morgan retorted, gesturing with a mottled leather portfolio case he was clutching in his left hand. "Thanks to you and that infernal meddling lover of yours, my entire operation has been jeopardized and my life has been threatened. How you've managed it, I've no idea, but it's left me with only one alternative—you. You're my ticket out of this; my ticket to a horse and provisions, and my tardy but eventual success."

"Clint won't…"

"He will, unless he wants to end up dead. Besides, how can he or anyone else stop me? You're not being abducted, after all; just consider yourself as being held hostage. And it's only for as long as it takes, then it's *hasta la vista*."

"You bastard!" I cried. "How dare you!" But my indignant fury never quite made it. Of course he would dare to; he would dare anything. He'd proven that enough times already.

My mind was churning. I edged slowly back from him, glaring so intently that even Morgan felt my fury and disgust. Not far from me was the desk. In its top desk drawer lay the pistol Clint had forced me to take. I had immediately put it away out of sight, positive I'd never have to use it, but this was one occasion which outweighed even my strong aversion to firearms.

If only I hadn't been so stupidly stubborn! Would I be able to reach it? As I turned toward the desk, Morgan stepped in front of me. I nearly escaped him again, ducking under his gnarled hands, but one of his massive arms whipped around my waist and he lifted me easily. I started to scream, but his ham-like hand clamped over my mouth. I struggled like a captive animal and Morgan's other hand curled into a rock-like fist and smashed against the side of my head. I felt my knees buckle as darkness surrounded me.

CHAPTER XIV

For a while, there was nothing, just a terrible, choking darkness. After a while I felt first heat, and then cold. I was haunted by one nightmare after another. There was sound and motion and the orange glow of fire filling my skull. I felt myself being picked up and held fast in the claws of a gigantic bird. Then I was falling from a tremendous distance. I watched, paralyzed and powerless, as the ground came up to meet me.

In reality, I was tied up in a burlap sack, being carted off to my own funeral. I heard an evil laugh and felt a jolt. I looked up to see a man in a black cowl-like robe waiting at the edge of an abyss. Slowly, menacingly, he removed his hood. The face was John Morgan's. As I looked down into the abyss, about to tumble into its depths, I saw my own image reflected back at me. My own hatred, my own anger, my own vengeance. Then I heard myself scream.

Instinctively, I realized this wasn't a dream. My eyelids felt leaden, too heavy to open. I was still in the sack, and my head ached with every jolt. I actually thought that I must be dead. Still, I forced my eyes open; then my nightmares spilled over into reality.

"I am truly sorry that it has to be this way." Morgan laughed contemptuously. His voice was unusually terse; he was obviously nervous and edgy. My ranting must have convinced him that holding me hostage would not secure his getaway as he'd anticipated. There would be no horse, no provisions, no safe passage, but he didn't seem to mind.

"Don't you see that this is for the best? I know you well enough to realize that you wouldn't have gone along with my plan without a struggle. The last thing I need is a hysterical woman slowing me down."

"And so you knocked me out?" My voice sounded thin. My head still ached, but I was beginning to think clearly again, even though I did not want to consider what might come next.

"It was the only way!" Morgan repeated. "You have always been such a thorn in my side. Did you think I would just let you and your husband take me prisoner?"

I answered him, my voice heavy and harsh. "Does Clint know you're alive? He won't let you get away with this!"

"Clint? Why my dear, it was your darling *Clint* who suggested it."

I turned my face away from him and closed my eyes, taking refuge behind the pain threatening to split my head in two. "No, not Clint!" my mind cried out. Then I remembered how adamant he had been about returning to Albuquerque. Without even talking to me first. Without taking me with him. Without even telling me good bye. Once he had set eyes on Maria again, had he changed his mind about where his heart lay? Was he now anxious to get me out of his life?

Morgan curled his lip up and put his hand on my shoulder. "Now, my dear, I'm going to leave you to die." He laughed again, pushing me down into the abyss. I gasped. Suddenly I was falling like I did in my worst nightmare.

I landed on something hard, but miraculously I survived. I ached all over, so I knew I wasn't dead, but it was still dark and scary.

Later, when the throbbing pain from the bump on my head had subsided, some of the self-possession I had once prided myself on came back to me. I found myself thinking more rationally. In my heart, I knew that Clint would never have abandoned me. I hugged that thought as I pondered my fate, and hope returned. Even though it seemed unlikely, I now believed that somehow Clint would come looking for me.

For a long time I remained utterly still. I managed to bring my knees to my chest and raise myself into a crouching position inside the burlap bag. I struggled to free myself. My fingers probed the sturdy cloth and closed on a hem of the burlap bag. With my arms restricted, the fold of material was too tough to tear, and I swore bitterly.

I twisted and groped as if I was confined in a straight jacket. I winced as the lance-like point of a sharp rock pierced the burlap and scratched my flesh. I began rubbing my body up and down across the rock until I finally heard the sack rip. I worked my fingers, then my arm, and finally my legs through the jagged tear. *Free at last!*

I lay still, trying to recover my strength and my wits. A fluttering sound filtered down from the cave roof. A colony of Mexican free-tailed bats bolted and veered away from the abyss. Then I heard another sound—the scraping of boots scuffing through gravel and rock.

I had landed on a rough ledge, maybe thirty feet across. Directly above, near the roof of the cave, was another ledge, a bit smaller in size. I must've rolled and slipped off it to my present position. A dusty ray of sunlight penetrated the cave through a narrow opening in the roof.

It took only a few minutes to orient myself. A voice, first just a whisper, reached my ears. I crept toward a crevasse in the wall at the back of the ledge and slipped into its darkness. On my hands and knees, I crawled down a crooked, sloping passage that emerged into an adjoining cave. I had barely stepped out of the narrow passageway when I heard the voices of two men entering the crevasse behind me. Morgan must have sent his henchmen to make sure I was dead.

Before I could contemplate my next move, a twisted human form wearing an Aurochs' skull reared up from behind and wildly shook its rattle at me. I knew instinctively that this must be the ancient shaman, Yellowhair. I dashed past him into the shadows and heard the men who had followed me curse angrily. I heard them come into the cave.

Then I heard Yellowhair's rattle again. The men rushed past him. Feeling my way along the sides of another passage, I fled deeper into the shadows, stumbling along until I was in absolute darkness. Fearing what might lie ahead, I moaned.

From some unseen source, a hint of light filtered down and softened the darkness. A honeycomb of crevasses, pockets and tunnels surrounded me. I realized that I must be in Devil's Canyon. Clint and Julio had described how a complex of caves riddled the cliffs.

I chose my course and ran, striking my left thigh on a projection of rock. I fell against the stone. The men were still following me, so I fled further until I found myself in another cavity. I stopped; no longer were the sounds coming from behind me. I crouched down.

Shaking with fright, I waited. Perhaps the men were searching elsewhere. I waited some more, scarcely breathing now. There was nobody in pursuit. Perhaps the intruders had gone. I gradually became convinced of this as the minutes passed. *I am finally safe*, I thought. Then I heard a sound from farther down another passage. To my horror, I also saw the flicker of flashlights.

I stood up cautiously. Groping frantically, I tried to find an opening somewhere in the rock wall. There was no escape; I had reached a dead end. It was as if I was entombed within a crypt.

I sank to my knees in the darkness and pressed the side of my face against the cool, granular surface which prevented my further advance. Rising, I turned around and leaned against the wall. I realized I had no choice but to go back the way I had come. Perhaps if I hid within the cover of shadows, I could slip past the men.

A hooded figure swung down from a rock slab. Landing six feet in front of me, he blocked my retreat. Behind me, another one dropped onto the floor of the cave. The one behind me was short, stocky, boar-like, and mean. The first one was bigger: about six-two, two hundred twenty pounds with a protruding gut hanging beneath the edge of his jacket. He stood there wielding a baseball bat as if it were a sledge-hammer. One of the old-fashioned hardwoods models. I knew they make a funny splat when they hit the ball. I didn't know the sound they made when they crushed a skull.

Oh shit! I thought. *You were right, Pierre. I shouldn't have come. I didn't need to prove how tough I was.*

"*Buenos días*, señorita!" the stocky man hissed at me. The man with the big belly was smacking his palm with the fat end of the bat. Who were these guys? What did they want? If they were trying to scare me, it was definitely working.

From the shadows, a terrifying figure emerged. Instinctively, I froze in horror. A parchment-covered face leered out beneath a horned, yellow-and-maroon feathered headdress. Naked save for the headdress and facial swathing, the gaunt and bony figure regarded me through slitted eyes. Mystic symbols covered its cheeks and body, ancient totems tattooed into the skin in agonizing rites, the result of deliberately inflicted wounds kept open and preserved with colored earth.

The figure's right fist clutched a bundle of withered cornstalks. In the left hand was a yellow rod surmounted with a cluster of feathers that matched the colors of the headdress and tattoos. A round pendant of hammered metal, about six inches in diameter, hung from a leather thong tied around the figure's neck. Incised into this pendant was the face of the same evil Kachina-like figure that stood before me—the *Chindi*, the devil of Navajo lore.

I was shocked at how the pendant was almost a living, breathing entity in itself. The eyes of the image on the disk opened and looked upon me with fury. From its mouth came a great cry of wrath. The naked figure responded in turn by raising the feathered rod threateningly above me. The men who had pursued me through the maze of tunnels and caves had fallen silent and now backed away in terror. Most of Morgan's collaborators, having bargained with the devil for their own evil intents and purposes, would not have cowered like the bat-wielding henchmen. Angered by their apparent cowardice, the imposing figure thrust the cluster of withered cornstalks into the faces of the men. They reacted by stepping closer behind me to block any chance of escape. Their demeanor became even more sinister as they stared down at me.

The slit-eyed figure now directed its attention toward me. A low, monotonous incantation rose from behind the mouthless parchment mask. The figure began to sway back and forth in a hypnotic rhythm. As though drawn by a magnetic force, the men shifted and swayed in unison with the fearsome figure. The chant droned on and on, resonating like the lowest tone on a pipe organ. The figure waved the feathered rod above my head like a maestro orchestrating a numbered opus—*Dances with Demons*.

Although I knew that the demon figure controlled the rod, it seemed to take on a life of its own. I felt myself being entranced by the perpetual hum of the incantation. The rod pulsed back and forth above me, as if trying to fetter out the scent of a trapped animal. I began to feel faint. Twice the rod hesitated and quivered directly over my head, alert to any sign of the devil's spawn: fear, hatred, or greed.

Worn out by the repetitive droning and swaying, I trembled. The rod, sensing my weakness, quivered like a stooping hawk ready to drop on its prey. The cry of a strangled rabbit spontaneously burst from my throat.

The *Chindi* countenance occupying the metal pendant instantly came to life. Fire burned within its eyes. A bone-chilling yowl rose into a high-pitched shriek. The deafening scream vibrated off every rock surface within the cave. Echo upon echo accelerated and amplified the piercing din. My teeth rattled. My bones ached. My skull felt ready to implode. I began to swoon. Grief, misery, hatred, and fear penetrated every cell of my body.

"Anything! I'll do anything to stop this agony!" I screamed. Then I crumpled to the floor, a glob of worthless humanity. My soul, the person I had been, was being extinguished, suffocated by the curse of primordial evil. Alone and abandoned, I no longer cared. I had fought enough. "Do what you will," I moaned.

I expected the worst, although my mind could not imagine what could be worse than this grating, tortuous assault. As life ebbed out of me, my whole body became racked with cold. Satisfied that I was beaten into submission, the disk's ghastly maw closed. The penetrating eyes failed to discern that deep in my heart, a final ember still burned. Released from the *Chindi's* noisy death howl, the spark flared.

Fed by love, the love of my family—my mother, my sons, my brother—my spirit revitalized. I heard Clayton's voice whisper to me. *"Don't give up, Sarah."* The flame grew even more. Warmth spread through me. I shuddered when I realized I had almost become a lifeless, hollow cavity. My senses quickly came back into focus. I lifted my head and gasped deeply. My body rose slowly as I emerged from the suffocation of primal fear. In a defiant voice I shouted out. "No! No! I will *not* succumb."

The background chant stopped. The feathered rod in the Kachina figure's left hand ceased its hypnotic rhythm and became an ordinary yellow stick. The towering figure uttered one last rumbling tone and indiscernible curse. The men, like the emaciated figure, stopped swaying. Two of them seized my arms and dragged me roughly across the cave floor toward the abyss.

No longer consumed by fear, I fought to free myself. Although I had discovered a new inner strength, it was not enough to stave off these brutes. Just when I began to realize that I had little hope of escaping a dreadful destiny at the hands of Morgan's henchmen, I saw a shadow leaping from rock to rock behind the men. With a blood-curdling whoop, Clint burst into the tunnel.

"Let her go!" Clint warned. "And that's not a mere suggestion; it's an *order*." The stocky man, who apparently was the enforcer, just laughed.

Clint said nothing in return, but his eyes bored holes through my captors. He bunched his forehead into little wrinkles and dropped into a straddle-leg stance, his hands moving threateningly in front of him.

It took all of two seconds for Clint to realize that he had bitten off more than he could chew. His opponent was built like a bull. He must have felt like an amateur rodeo cowboy who had unwittingly leaped onto the back of a bucking bull; he was holding on for dear life as the two of them wrestled wildly.

The sheer power of the man was terrifying. His two huge, viselike hands managed to close around Clint's head. For a few moments, I feared he wasn't going to survive the ordeal. Only animal instinct saved him from having his brains turned into mush.

The assailant's beefy wrist slipped lower onto Clint's jaw. He twisted his head and somehow managed to stretch his mouth open wide enough to clamp around flesh and wristbone. Then he gave a mighty chomp. With a painful bellow, the assailant released his grip. Clint slid down and grabbed the baseball bat lying on the ground. In desperation, he took hold of the small end and smacked the henchman in the face.

"It would appear," Julio said, "that I have arrived in the proverbial nick of time." He burst through the tunnel opening behind him.

"What the hell took you so long? Am I ever glad to see you!" Clint answered excitedly.

"Looks like I made it in time for the ninth inning."

Clint's eyebrows rose. "I was getting really worried. Usually you know when I'm in trouble long before this."

"Shall we cut these guys' balls off?" Julio smirked, looking at the gorilla of a man who kept smacking his hand on the fat end of the bat.

"Sure. But we'd better hurry up before we find ourselves attacked by any more of Morgan's creeps."

Julio's threat unnerved my former captors. The one Clint had hit with the bat rubbed his jaw. Then both of them fled into a tunnel.

"Those guys have been subdued for the time being, but that doesn't mean we're out of danger," Julio warned as he watched the men disappear into the shadows.

For the first time since my capture, I had a chance to look carefully at our surroundings. "What happened to the Kachina figure with the *Chindi* medallion on its chest?" Neither Clint nor Julio understood my question. They shrugged as though they thought I had been hallucinating, and began discussing their game plan.

Julio glanced toward the stone corridor and spotted three dark forms making their way through the tunnel. "We'd better get out of here, pronto," he said, scurrying toward the front of the chamber. "Over here." He motioned to us as we ducked behind a boulder next to a shallow, stagnant pool.

A palsy rippled across my shoulders and down my arms at the possibility of another violent confrontation. The three hooded figures stood at the mouth of the tunnel and began searching the chamber with their flashlights. I sucked in my breath at the sight of the *Chindi's* evil pawns—John Morgan and his henchmen.

Clint's lips curled into a fierce grin. "So do we disappoint them and cut and run?"

"Since when were we ever smart enough to take the easy way out?"

"Never, that I recall."

Clint's bond with Julio had never weakened in all their years of friendship—a friendship that went all the way back to their training as Navy test pilots. That they worked as a close-knit team went without saying. Whatever scheme was devised, no matter how insane or ridiculous, they were in it for the action. When required, they could also get inside each other's head. They had saved each other's life on more than one occasion, and their adventures had become legendary within the U.S. Naval Academy.

"It would be almost impossible for both of us to rush in unison before they react," Julio said, eyeing the narrow tunnel opening. "We could climb over a ledge, drop down, and knife them in their respective guts. If our positions were reversed," he murmured so softly that Clint could barely hear him, "that's what they would do to us. But the ethical side of me says to take them alive."

"Easier said than done."

Having experienced Morgan's almost supernatural resiliency, I found the prospect of victory unlikely. In view of the power that Clint and Julio were facing, I just could not imagine a favorable outcome. With a spiteful determination to compel us into showing ourselves, the leader of the hooded forms planted himself solidly and taunted us to draw us out into the open.

"I'll never stand trial!" Morgan shouted.

His twisted sense of victory became evident when he opened his black hooded jacket. There was a pipe bomb around his waist. Clint knocked Julio and me to the ground just as he reached to fire the detonator. He shielded my body with his own. A wave of nausea engulfed me as the vortex of the blast swept over us.

When the dust settled, the three of us crawled out from behind the rock. As a shadowy curtain parted, our mouths dropped open at the sight of the three torn and bloodied bodies.

"That dude shouldn't have been trusted with explosives," Clint quipped, nodding his head toward Morgan.

The blistered, shapeless bundles of flesh no longer had the semblance of human faces. A piece of shrapnel had removed the lower jaw of one man. The scrap of flesh hanging from the wound did not hide the trachea through which his breath escaped in bubbles; it was accompanied by a kind of gurgling. The force from the explosion had threshed the shoulder and arm of another man into pulp. His skin had been torn away and his blood seemed to be running out through several pipes.

"I have twenty-five enemy combat sorties to my credit, but I have never seen anything to equal this," Clint grimaced.

Neither a cry nor a moan escaped the lips of the wounded. Even though these monstrous supermen were dying, they somehow rose and flung themselves forward. The man without a jaw could scarcely stand. The one-armed man clung to a stone ledge with his other skinless, bleeding arm. Eventually both crumpled slowly to the ground. Morgan tried to rise, holding in his guts with one hand and stretching out the other with a gesture of tormented pain. The flow of blood from the three bodies spread into an ever-increasing stream that settled into the stagnant pool.

The three of us stood there looking at the grisly aftermath. I had thought that the gardener dangling from the gated spire was one of the most traumatic things I had ever seen, but this topped everything. I stared at Morgan's body. Something compelled me to make sure he was dead. I walked over to push him with my foot, then I reached down to feel for a pulse.

"He's dead," I said at last. "This evil man is finally dead." Still in shock from the mutilation and carnage that littered the cave, I apprehensively searched the shadowed recesses for any sign of the terrifying *Chindi*. Nothing stirred.

I looked at Clint and Julio. "Is it really over?"

Clint came over and took me in his arms. "Sarah, you're free from the curse of the *Chindi*. No one is going to hurt you ever again. Thank God we were able to get here in time and save you. I will never let anything separate us again. We need to contact Estes and the authorities to explain what just happened."

Julio took my hand. "Come *Shi-da-zii*, let's leave this place."

We made our way back to the cabin. Fortunately Clint's cell phone still worked. Estes and his men were on the way to take care of the dead. He was grateful that Morgan had finally been found.

Later on, Julio sat down beside me. "You were mistaken if you thought Clint turned his back on you because of some secret passion he had for his old flame, Maria. I don't think he is capable of loving any woman as strongly as he loves you."

Tongue-tied, I remained silent. I felt the knot that was already in my stomach tightening as he leaned over and whispered to me. "Maria Venezuela is a very powerful medicine woman. Some say she controls the wind."

"You don't have to convince *me*. Look at the power she has over Clint!" I had known she was a medicine woman when Little Dove first described her to me when we were picking berries. From what she said, Maria seemed to have animalistic instincts about her. I didn't trust her, that was for sure.

"She made you curious," he continued. "And I was curious, too. When Clint came back to our camp looking like a man in a daze, I was curious enough to sit outside the shaman's lodge and listen while he told my father of the conversations he'd had with Maria. 'I cannot save her,' he'd said. His voice held such anguish that I hardly recognized it. But later that same night, Maria came, her hair flying behind her in the storm wind and her face haggard—as haggard as *his* had been. 'You must save her,' she'd cried. I can still hear her now. 'You must fight the demons of the underworld and not allow them to capture Sarah!'"

Julio paused meaningfully, as if he expected me to say something, but I could only stare back at him silently. "You know the rest of it, I think," he said quietly.

I shuddered. "He overcame the dark forces, but was it blood for blood? Or was it his own guilt that made him risk his life so carelessly?"

Julio smiled faintly at my chagrined expression. "Clint's only concern is for your happiness, *Shi-da-zii*. And I am relieved to know that he is the person who saved your life. You see, *Shi-da-zii*? You are the Little Yellow Bird in his dream."

Suddenly I realized the real reason for Clint's recent emotional distance. Maria was not some master manipulator in all our lives, but she exercised a subtle fascination, a subtle power, and it seemed as if only Clint had been affected by her powers. She may have predicted my capture, but I was glad I didn't know her. I had no desire to make her acquaintance.

Clint's face came into my mind with a jolt. How long had it been since I had thought about him without feeling angry or jealous of Maria? Had I deliberately tried to push him away from me because I was afraid of losing him? If only I had listened to the shaman. If only I had paid more attention to Julio's observations! A memory of Clint kissing me and crushing me in his embrace came unbidden to my mind.

That night after dinner, Clint lit a fire, turned on the radio and tuned in some romantic music. It was good to be back at the cabin. He motioned me over to where he was standing. I walked over and threw my arms around his neck. I pressed myself up against him, then rocked back and forth on my tiptoes as we began swaying with the music. "I'm so sorry that I didn't trust you."

I looked up at him with loving eyes. I longed to stay in his embrace all night. His neck was fragrant with the seductive musky scent of his favorite cologne. My hands slid down his back to his round, tight bottom. He was so athletic and muscular.

Then he pulled me toward him, looking at me through his sexy green eyes. "You're a wonderful woman," he said, straining against me and running his hands across my back. "More woman than I deserve."

"You're my hero," I murmured as I held him close.

"I never want to let you out of my sight again," he said as he picked me up and took long strides into the bedroom.

On our last day in Hidden Valley, Clint and I took a hike. We scaled Mount Negro, the butte that nestles against Devil's Canyon. When we reached the top, we held hands and looked down on what represented more than a decade of hell. Before leaving, we placed a rock on the summit, commemorating our trench warfare with the avatars of evil—the *Chindi*.

We inscribed the dates "August 1991 to August 2002" on the rock. It represented the time frame from when I was first plunged into this dark odyssey to its resolution. Destiny had brought Clint and me together through the death of my brother and the death of his wife. We had then been cast into an even deeper darkness together, only to find ourselves defeating evil and finding love.

On the back of the rock, Clint wrote, "We won."

ABOUT THE AUTHOR

Following her love of adventure, Sandra Fendler traveled extensively as a former flight attendant. She also has a successful business background and has operated a variety of enterprises including a gift shop where she bought and sold works created by Navajo artists.

An Arizona resident for forty-five years, Sandra currently resides in a small community where she enjoys nature, wildlife, and an outdoor lifestyle that inspires her writing. *Dance of the Demon* is her second mystery novel.

The sequel to *Curse of the Chindi, Dance of the Demon* continues the theme of Fendler's first book, which is based on a true murder mystery within the Navajo Reservation. The author has written a series of mystery novels that incorporate cultural traditions and geographic landscapes of Arizona and western New Mexico. Her third book, *She-Devil Shenanigans,* touches upon facts related to the initial murder but then evolves into a purely fictional tale revolving around mystical Native American beliefs. A fourth book, *White Wolf Woman's Wrath,* is a metaphor for the demons, whether real or imagined, that have plagued the series' heroine, Sarah Simms. In the fifth book, *Jade-Eyed Jaguar,* the heroine banishes culprits and demons once and for all to complete the *Curse of the Chindi* series.

ABOUT THE ARTIST

Artist Rock Newcomb was raised on a ranch in southern Idaho and began drawing at the age six. He earned his B.A. and M.A. in Art from California State University, Fullerton. He taught art in the public sector prior to focusing on a fulltime, professional art career.

His award-winning work has been featured in several public exhibitions, including the Smithsonian Institution, Swedish Museum of Natural History, National Cowboy & Western Heritage Museum, Leigh Yawkey Woodson Art Museum, the Briscoe Western Art Museum, and the Eiteljorg Museum of American Indians and Western Art. PBS Television also chose Newcomb as a demonstration artist for the "Artists Workshop" series.

His work is represented by Astoria Fine Art, Jackson, Wyoming; Huey's Fine Art, Santa Fe, New Mexico; Legacy Gallery, Scottsdale, Arizona and Bozeman, Montana, and Lord Nelson's Gallery, Gettysburg, Pennsylvania. Newcomb's art also hangs in corporate and private collections throughout the United States and abroad.

He resides in Payson, Arizona, with his wife and business manager, Cody Newcomb.

Inquiries about the artwork featured on the book cover, and other available artwork, should be directed to the artist at www.cody.rocknewcomb@gmail.com